A MANUAL BOOK OF HISTOLOGY
组织学实习指导（英文版）

Editor-in-Chief Zou Zhongzhi
主　编　邹仲之

U0128829

Editors（编　者）

Dong Weiren （Southern Medical University）
董为人　（南方医科大学）
Li He (Tongji Medical College, Huazhong University of Science and Technology)
李　和　（华中科技大学同济医学院）
Qi Jianguo (West China School of Preclinical and Forensic Medicine, Sichuan University)
齐建国　（四川大学华西基础医学与法医学院）
Wang Zhanyou （China Medical University）
王占友　（中国医科大学）
Wen Jianguo (Xiangya School of Medicine, Central South University)
文建国　（中南大学湘雅医学院）
Xu Chen （Medical College, Shanghai Jiao Tong University）
徐　晨　（上海交通大学医学院）
Zeng Yuanshan (Zhongshan School of Medicine, Sun Yat-sen University)
曾园山　（中山大学中山医学院）
Zhong Cuiping （Shanghai Medical College, Fudan University）
钟翠平　（复旦大学上海医学院）
Zhou Li （Bethune Medical College, Jilin University）
周　莉　（吉林大学白求恩医学部）
Zou Zhongzhi （Southern Medical University）
邹仲之　（南方医科大学）

English Editor　（英文编辑）

Manas Das

人民卫生出版社

图书在版编目(CIP)数据

组织学实习指导(英文版)/邹仲之主编. —北京:
人民卫生出版社,2008.11
ISBN 978 - 7 - 117 - 10661 - 0

Ⅰ. 组⋯　Ⅱ. 邹⋯　Ⅲ. 人体组织学 - 医学院校 -
教学参考资料 - 英文　Ⅳ. R329

中国版本图书馆 CIP 数据核字(2008)第 149323 号

组织学实习指导（英文版）

A MANUAL BOOK OF HISTOLOGY

主　　编:邹仲之
出版发行:人民卫生出版社(中继线 010 - 67616688)
地　　址:北京市丰台区方庄芳群园 3 区 3 号楼
邮　　编:100078
网　　址:http:// www. pmph. com
E - mail:pmph @ pmph. com
购书热线:010 - 67605754　010 - 65264830
印　　刷:北京人卫印刷厂
经　　销:新华书店
开　　本:787 × 1092　1/16　　印张:6.25
字　　数:155 千字
版　　次:2008 年 11 月第 1 版　2008 年 11 月第 1 版第 1 次印刷
标准书号:ISBN 978 - 7 - 117 - 10661 - 0/R·10662
定　　价:45.00 元

▶ 插图说明

一、提供单位及作者（按单位拼音为序；无特殊说明，均为各校组胚教研室）：

　　复旦大学上海医学院（简称复旦上医；钟翠平、周国民）

　　河北北方学院基础医学部（简称河北北方医；周济远、任君旭）

　　华中科技大学同济医学院（李和）

　　吉林大学白求恩医学部（简称吉大白医；周莉、尹昕、朱秀雄）

　　广州医学院（马宁芳）

　　南方医科大学（简称南方医；邹仲之、傅俊贤、田雪梅、董为人、晏芳）

　　上海交通大学医学院（简称上交大医）

　　四川大学华西基础医学与法医学院（齐建国、保天然、廖德阳）

　　中南大学湘雅医学院（文建国）

　　中山大学中山医学院（曾园山、李海标）

二、凡未注明染色方法的组织切片标本图，均为 HE 染色。

三、未经图作者授权，不得擅自应用于任何出版物。

CONTENTS

Chapter 11 Skin

Chapter 12 Immune System

Chapter 13 Endocrine System

Chapter 14 Digestive Tract

Chapter 15 Digestive glands

Chapter 16 Respiratory System

Chapter 17 Urinary System

Chapter 18 Male Reproductive System

Chapter 19 Female Reproductive System

Chapter 1

Preface

1. As a Chinese saying "百闻不如一见" says, "Seeing it once is better than hearing about it a hundred times", it is indispensable in the study of histology to observe histological specimens under microscope. It benefits the learners to understand and remember histological theories, to obtain the abilities to observe objects and to describe the observed objects.

2. To observe a specimen, at first, the observer should have a look at its general features with the naked eyes, to see whether it is a parenchymal or a hollow organ. For the parenchymal organs, he should use the low magnifying lenses (4 × and 10 ×) to scan the whole specimen from its surface inwards to identify the different areas, and then use the high magnifying lens (40 ×) to observe the delicate structures and cells. For the hollow organs, the order of observation is from the inside to the surface.

3. Despite the 3-D structure of the observed objects, the specimens provide only flat images. So the observer should revert in mind the 2-dimensional figures of the organ, tissue and cells to their 3-dimensional structures. Furthermore, sections of the same kind of cells, tissue or an organ can appear different because of the directions of sectioning (transverse, longitudinal, oblique and tangential sections) (Fig.1-1).

4. The morphology of the same kind of structures can appear different because of different physiological conditions. So the observer should associate the morphology of a structure with its function.

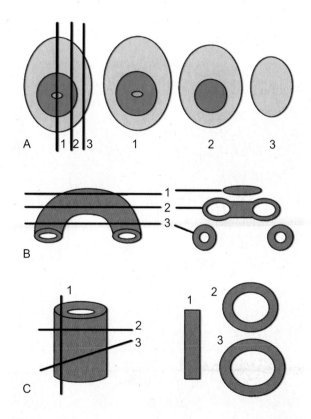

Fig. 1-1 the relationship between the three-dimensional structures and the two-dimensional sections
A. Sections of a cell. 1. passing through cytoplasm, nucleus and nucleolus; 2. passing through cytoplasm and nucleus; 3. passing through cytoplasm. B. Sections of a curved vessel. 1. tangental section; 2. passing through the curved part; 3. passing through the separated part. C. Sections of a straight vessel. 1. tangental section; 2. transverse section; 3. oblique section

5. The preparation of specimens often leave some traces in the sections such as clefts, folds, knife traces, dyes and even dirt.

6. To draw histological illustrations, one should select the typical structures, note their morphology, position and the ratio of the sizes. Generally, the basophilic structures (i.e., nuclei) are drawn with a blue pencil, and the eosinophilic (i.e., cytoplasm, collagen fibers) structures with a red pencil. The shades of the colors should be noted. The names of the structures in the illustrations should be marked.

7. For microphotography, one should select the typical structures, and balance the locations of the structures, the focus, the brightness and the real color.

8. The following abbreviations are used in the text: transverse section-TS; longitudinal section-LS; hematoxylin-eosin-HE; naked eyes-NE; low magnifying lens-LMag; high magnifying lens-HMag.

Appendix: The structures and operation of a microscope
Main components of a microscope (Fig. 1-2)

1. Power switch.

2. Light control, used to adjust the brightness of the field of vision in eyepieces.

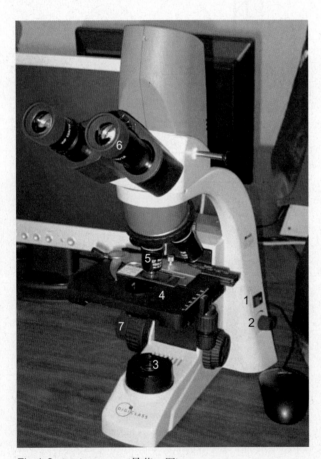

3. Light source.

4. Stage. The slide can be held tightly by the holder on the stage and be moved by the slide driver at one side of the stage.

5. Objective lenses. Generally 3 lenses of different magnification ($4 \times$, $10 \times$ and $40 \times$) are used on the revolving nosepiece.

6. Condenser and iris diaphragm (Fig.1-3E). The condenser concentrates the light onto the specimen. The iris diaphragm is housed in the condenser, it works to control the diameter of the light beam, or to adjust the brightness of the field of vision.

7. Focal adjustments (Fig.1-3F). Generally, the coarse adjustment can be used when $4 \times$ or $10 \times$ lens is used; the fine adjustment for $40 \times$ lens.

8. Eyepieces. Generally, their magnification is $10 \times$. The distance between the two pieces is adjusted by pushing them outward or inward.

Operation of a microscope

Fig.1-2 A microscope (晏芳 图)

1. power switch; 2. light control; 3. light source; 4. stage; 5. objective lens; 6. eyepieces; 7. focal adjustments

Preparations:

1. Take off the cover of the microscope,

fold it and put it into the drawer, then take out the specimen box (To keep the slides from dust, close the specimen box except when taking out slides from it).

2. Move the microscope to a proper position in front of the observer.

3. Adjust the height of the stool to ensure a comfortable observation.

Procedure:

1. Turn on the power switch.

2. Take out a slide from the specimen box, have a look at the shape and the color of the section with naked eyes; put the slide on the stage (make the coverslip upward; center the section with the slide driver) (Fig.1-3A、B).

3. Determine the lens (To observe a slide, always use 4 × objective at first, then 10 × and 40 ×) (Fig. 1-3C).

4. Adjust the distance between the two eyepieces to suit the observer's eyes.

5. Adjust the brightness with the light control (Fig.1-3D) and sometimes the iris diaphragm until a desired contrast is obtained (Fig.1-3E).

6. Focus the image with the focus adjustments (firstly coarse adjustment, then fine adjustment) (Fig. 1-3F).

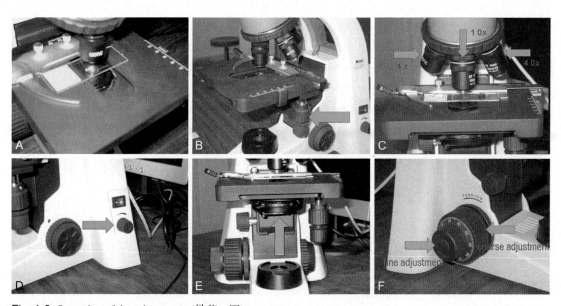

Fig. 1-3 Operation of the microscope (晏芳　图)

Change the specimen:

1. Change the lens to 4 × objective.

2. Take the observed slide off the stage and put it back into the specimen box.

3. Take out another slide from the box, observe it with naked eyes, and then put it on the stage.

4. Focus the image with fine adjustment.

Complete the observation (before the class is over) :

1. Decrease the brightness to the minimum with the light control.

2. Turn off the power switch.

3. Get the slides properly stored (the slide in the box and the box in the drawer).

4. Cover the microscope and store it at the former place.

(by Zou Zhongzhi)

Chapter 2

Epithelial Tissue

1. Simple squamous epithelium (endothelium, TS of medium-sized artery and vein)

Specimen No._____ Fig. 2-1

Preparation: HE stain

NE The medium-sized artery has a smaller and relatively round lumen while the medium-sized vein has a larger and relatively irregular lumen.

LMag Observe the endothelial lining of the inner surface of the vessel wall. Due to contraction of the artery, the endothelium appears wave-like. On the other hand, the epithelium of the vein appears relatively smooth.

HMag The pink stained cytoplasm of endothelial cells is so thin that it is difficult to distinguish them from the pink connective tissue which is beneath them and continuous. The nuclei of endothelial cells, which are stained blue, slightly bulge towards the lumen.

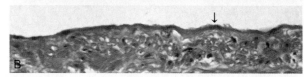

Fig. 2-1 Simple squamous epithelium (南方医 图)
A. medium-sized artery. B. medium-sized vein. ↓ nucleus of the epithelial cell

2. Simple columnar epithelium (gall bladder)

Specimen No._____ Fig. 2-2

Preparation: HE stain

NE The uneven part of the specimen is the mucosa of the gall bladder wall, which has numerous plicae and is stained blue. The other parts of the gall bladder wall are stained pink.

LMag Find the mucosal plicae and the surfaces of the plicae lined with simple columnar epithelium.

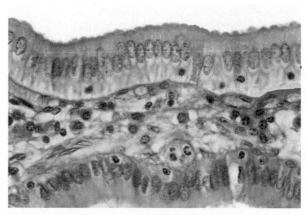

Fig. 2-2 Simple columnar epithelium (gall bladder) (南方医 图)

HMag The epithelium consists of tall columnar cells; their nuclei are elongated and are located towards the base; the cytoplasm is pink.

3. Simple columnar epithelium (jejunum)

Specimen No._____ Fig. 2-3

Preparation: HE stain

NE One side of the specimen is unevenly blue-stained and has numerous fingerlike mucosal projections called intestinal villi. The other side is stained pink.

LMag Find the intestinal villi and observe their longitudinal, transverse and oblique sections. The transverse and oblique sections are usually isolated from the intestinal wall. The surface of the villi is coated by simple columnar epithelium. Goblet cells are scattered among the columnar cells.

HMag

(1) Columnar cells: Columnar cells are tall and columnar in perpendicular section. The nuclei are oval, located in the cell base. The striated border, a deep red structure that is uniformly thin, can be seen along the free surface of the cells.

Fig. 2-3 Simple columnar epithelium (small intestine)(李和　图)

1. columnar cell; 2. goblet cell; ← striated border

(2) Goblet cells: Goblet cells are scattered among the columnar cells, resembling a goblet in shape. The basal part of the cell is narrow, containing a darkly stained nucleus which is triangular or oblate in shape. The extensive apical portion of the cell is filled with mucinogen granules, usually vacuolated because they are lightly stained; but in some sections, its apical portion is blue.

The lymphocytes are often found among epithelial cells; their nuclei are small and round and stained dark blue.

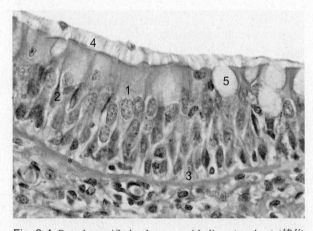

Fig. 2-4 Pseudostratified columnar epithelium (trachea) (傅俊贤　图)

1. columnar cell; 2. fusiform cell; 3. pyramidal cell (basal cell); 4. cilia; 5. goblet cell; * basement membrane

4. Pseudostratified ciliated columnar epithelium (trachea, TS)

Specimen No._____ Fig. 2-4

Preparation: HE stain

NE The innermost layer of the tracheal

wall, which is stained blue, is lined with pseudostratified ciliated columnar epithelium.

LMag Find the luminal surface of the trachea and identify the pseudostratified ciliated columnar epithelium. The epithelial cells are so closely arranged that the borders are difficult to identify. The nuclei of the epithelial cells are disposed at different levels, thus creating the appearance of stratified epithelium. The goblet cells are found scattered among other cells.

HMag

(1) Columnar cells (ciliated cells): They are numerous in number, tall columnar in shape with an extensive apex reaching the luminal surface. Their nuclei are ellipsoidal, usually located in the upper portion or the superficial layer of the epithelium. The cytoplasm is pink. The free surfaces of the cells are densely and regularly arranged with small thin projections called cilia.

(2) Fusiform cells: They are dispersed among other cells. Its soma is fusiform with an indistinct limit. Its narrowly ellipsoidal and centrally positioned nucleus is located in the middle layer of the epithelium.

(3) Pyramidal cells (basal cells): They are located in base of the epithelium. They are small with an apex embedded in other cells. The nuclei are round, arranged in the deep layer of the epithelium.

(4) Goblet cells: They are similar to the intestinal goblet cells in morphology. These cells are scattered in the epithelium and extend through the entire thickness of the epithelium.

(5) Basement membrane: It is a distinct, thin, homogeneous and pink stained membrane beneath the epithelium.

5. Stratified squamous epithelium (esophagus, TS)

Specimen No._____ Fig. 2-5

Preparation: HE stain

NE The blue stained layer of the esophageal luminal surface is stratified squamous epithelium.

LMag The epithelium is composed of multiple layers of densely arranged cells. The connective tissue under the epithelium forms many papillary projections into it, which makes an uneven interface between them. The obliquely sectioned connective papillae appear as pale stained structures in the epithelium.

HMag Observe the epithelial cells in each layer from base to the surface.

(1) Basal layer: It is composed of a layer of low columnar cells which have round nuclei. The basophilia of the cytoplasm is stronger than that of cells in any other layer.

(2) Intermediate layer: It contains several layers of polygonal cells. The cells near the superficial layer become fusiform. The nuclei of the cells in this layer are oval or

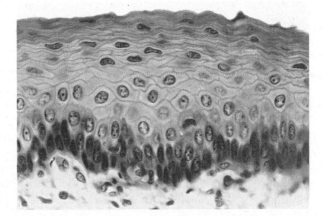

Fig. 2-5 Stratified squamous epithelium (esophagus)
(河北北方医　图)

round and centrally located.

(3) Superficial layer: The cells in this layer are squamous, each containing a small flattened nucleus. Some of the cells tend to be separated from the underlying cells.

6. Transitional epithelium (urinary bladder)

Specimen No.____ Fig. 2-6, Fig. 2-7

Preparation: HE stain

NE There are two sections on the slide, the thin is the section of the distended bladder wall while the thick the section of the empty bladder wall. The even and blue stained side of each section is transitional epithelium.

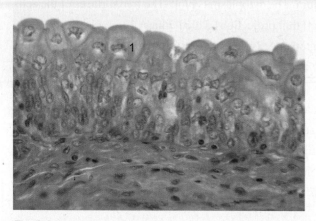

Fig. 2-6 Transitional epithelium (urinary bladder, empty state) (南方医　图)

1. superficial cell

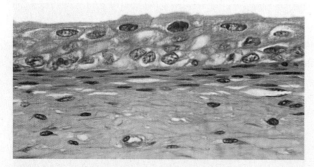

Fig. 2-7 Transitional epithelium (urinary bladder, distended state) (南方医　图)

LMag

(1) Empty state: The epithelium is thick, containing 4 to 5 layers of cells.

(2) Distended state: The epithelium is thin, containing 2 to 3 layers of cells.

HMag

(1) Empty state: The cells of the superficial layer are large and thick in size, cuboidal or rectangular in shape, having 1 ~ 2 nuclei. One superficial cell can cover several cells in the intermediate layer. The intermediate layer contains several layers of polygonal cells. The basal layer contains one layer of cuboidal or low columnar cells.

(2) Distended state: Most cells of the three layers become flattened while the superficial cells are the most prominent.

7. Mixed gland (submandibular gland)

Specimen No.____ Fig. 2-8

Preparation: HE stain

NE The organ is separated into many blue pieces.

LMag Numerous round, oval or irregular sections of acini and ducts of unequal sizes are seen. The staining of the acini is uneven. The serous acini appear as dark staining bodies, the mucous acini pale staining bodies, and the mixed acini pale or dark staining bodies.

HMag

(1) Acini: Each acinus is composed of several glandular cells which surround a central lumen. Some of the acini are continuous with their ducts.

1) Serous acini: Each serous acinus comprises several serous cells and a small central lumen. The nuclei of serous cells are round and are located in the central or basal region. The cytoplasm of the basal region is blue due to strong basophilia; that of the apical region usually contains a lot of red zymogen granules.

2) Mucous acini: The mucous acini, formed by mucous cells, are larger than the serous acini. The basal, oblate nuclei of mucous cells are deeply stained. Small amount of perinuclear cytoplasm is basophilic and stained blue, and the remaining cytoplasm is poorly stained, being foamy or vacuolated.

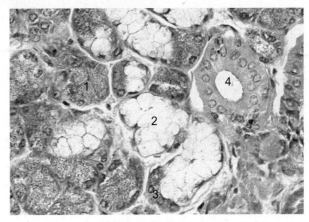

Fig. 2-8 Submandibular gland (钟翠平　图)
1. serous acinus; 2. mucous acinus; 3. serous demilune; 4. striated duct

3) Mixed acini: They are made up of serous and mucous cells. Most of the mixed acini are made up of mucous cells, but serous cells constitute a cap on one side or at the bottom of the acinus. The cap of serous cells looks like a crescent moon, hence known as a serous demilune.

In addition, flattened myoepithelial cells are seen surrounding the basal surfaces of the acini, the nuclei of which are flat and deeply stained.

(2) Ducts: The ducts, which have obvious lumina, are composed of simple cuboidal or columnar cells. The cytoplasm of the epithelial cells is pink.

(by Li He)

Chapter 3

Connective Tissue

1. Loose connective tissue (rat mesentery)

Specimen No.＿＿＿ Fig. 3-1, Fig. 3-2

Preparation: Rat mesentery is sampled several hours after intraperitoneal injection of trypan blue, and then stretched and mounted on the slide. Special stain is applied.

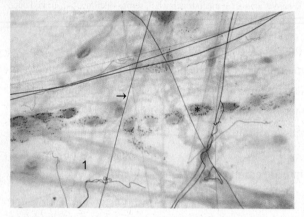

Fig. 3-1 Loose connective tissue (spread of rat mesentery; intraperitoneal injection of trypan blue, special stain to show elastic fiber) (南方医 图)

1. collagenous fiber; * macrophage; → elastic fiber

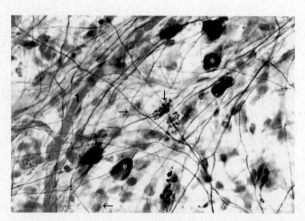

Fig. 3-2 Loose connective tissue (spread of rat mesentery; intraperitoneal injection of trypan blue, special stain to show mast cell and elastic fiber) (南方医 图)

1. capillary; * mast cell; ↓ macrophage; ← fibroblast; → elastic fiber

LMag Because of the uneven thickness of the mesentery, it is recommended to select thinner and lightly stained areas of the mesentery for observation by constantly manipulating the fine adjustment knob. A lot of deeply stained cells, fine fibers and pale pink amorphous ground substance can be seen. Blood capillaries containing red blood cells are also found.

HMag

(1) Macrophages: They are mostly oval and characterized by coarse trypan blue granules unevenly dispersed in the cytoplasm and by small oval nucleus.

(2) Mast cells: They are round or oval, and usually found in groups. Their nuclei are round or oval, centrally located. They are characterized by deep-staining granules in the cytoplasm. The individual granules cannot be easily identified because of their intensive aggregation.

(3) Fibroblasts: They are most abundant and large, with fluffy boundary and a few processes. Their nuclei are ovoid, large, and pale staining, with prominent nucleoli. The cytoplasm is abundant and weakly basophilic.

Small amounts of trypan blue granules can be seen in the cytoplasm.

(4) Collagen fibers: They are abundant and appear as thick, pink strings with some branches. They cross each other to form a meshwork.

(5) Elastic fibers: They are thin and purple stained by aldehyde-fuchsin. They tend to have more even diameter although they branch sometimes. They usually have curling ends.

2. Plasma cells (trachea, TS)

Specimen No.____ Fig. 3-3

Preparation: HE stain

LMag Loose connective tissue is just underlying the luminal epithelium.

HMag Plasma cells can be identified in the loose connective tissue. They are large, round or ovoid cells that have a basophilic cytoplasm with a pale juxta nuclear area. The nucleus of a plasma cell is spherical and eccentrically placed, containing compact, coarse heterochromatin radiating from the center of the nucleus to the peripheral nuclear envelope, which is commonly described as a clock-face appearance.

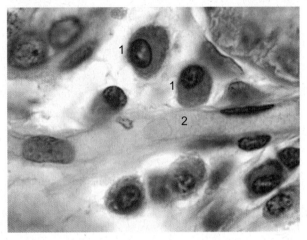

Fig. 3-3 Plasma cells (tracheal mucosa) (南方医　图)
1. plasma cell; 2. capillary

3. Dense irregular connective tissue and adipose tissue (skin of finger)

Specimen No.____ Fig. 3-4, Fig. 3-5

Preparation: HE stain

NE The epidermis (keratinized stratified squamous epithelium) contains a cardinal red superficial portion and a blue deeper portion. The dermis, the underlying pink layer, is mainly made up of dense irregular connective tissue. The deepest and the lightest layer beneath the dermis is hypodermis, or adipose tissue.

LMag Large amounts of pink collagen fibers are present in the dermis. They run at different directions to form a meshwork, showing in longitudinal, transverse and oblique sections. Artifacts in the spaces between these fibers can be seen. Move the slide to the deeper portion to define the

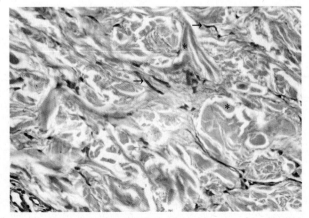

Fig. 3-4 Dense irregular connective tissue (dermis) (董为人　图)
→ fibrocyte; * collagenous fiber

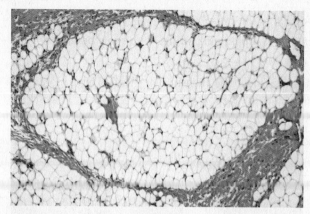

Fig. 3-5 Adipose tissue (南方医 图)

adipose tissue. Adipocytes appear in groups separated by loose connective tissue and form lots of fat lobules.

HMag

(1) Dense irregular connective tissue: Some fibroblasts and fibrocytes are dispersed in collagen fiber bundles, which are identified mainly by the appearance of the nuclei because of their obscure outlines. Fibroblasts have pale, larger, ovoid nuclei while fibrocytes have dark, small, fusiform nuclei.

(2) Adipocytes: An adipocyte appears as a thin ring of pink cytoplasm surrounding a large vacuole, because the lipid droplets have been dissolved during histological preparation. Consequently, the cell has an eccentric and flattened nucleus.

4. Dense regular connective tissue (tendon, LS & TS)

Specimen No.____ Fig. 3-6

Preparation: HE stain

NE LS of the tendon is long while the TS is round.

Microscope

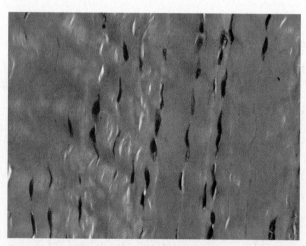

Fig. 3-6 Dense regular connective tissue (tendon, LS) (晏芳 图)

LS : There are numerous condensed pink collagen fiber bundles in parallel array with fibrocytes among the fibers at low magnification. At high magnification, the fibrocyte has an elongated and dark nucleus, and very little detail about the cytoplasm is visible.

TS : Fibrocytes are seen dispersed among transected collagen fibers of various diameters at low magnification. At high power, fibrocyte is star-shaped with a spherical nucleus and several thin wing-like processes inserting into the fibers.

5. Reticular tissue (lymph node)

Specimen No.____ Fig. 3-7

Preparation: silver stain

NE The lymph node is a brownish-black, kidney-shaped organ. Reticular tissue can be easily detected in lightly stained areas.

LMag Reticular fibers appear black and thin. They have branches that cross with each other to form an extensive network. **HMag** Reticular cells are stellate cells with many cytoplasmic processes attached to reticular fibers. They have large round or ovoid nuclei with prominent nucleoli. The cytoplasm is stained pale.

(by Dong Weiren)

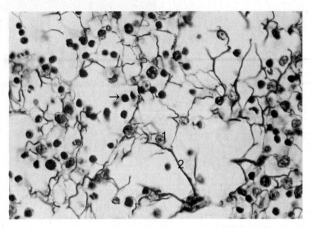

Fig. 3-7 Reticular tissue (lymph node; silver stain) (河北北方医　图)
1. reticulocyte (nucleus); 2. reticular fiber; → lymphocyte

Chapter 4

Blood

Blood smear

Specimen No.____ Fig. 4-1 ~ Fig. 4-6

Preparation: Wright or Giemsa stain

NE Blood is spread on the slide to form a thin, pink film. Select thin and even areas for observation.

LMag There are numerous spherical, pink, anucleated erythrocytes, interspersed with larger, polymorphous leukocytes with darkly stained nuclei.

HMag (immersion objective can be used)

(1) Erythrocytes: They are small spherical cells with a darker periphery and a lighter center. They have no nucleus.

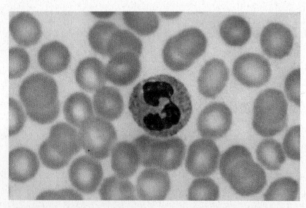

Fig. 4-1 A neutrophil and red blood cells (南方医　图)

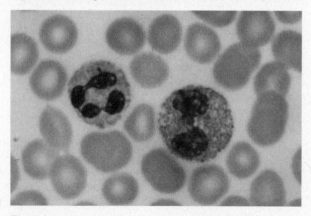

Fig. 4-2 A neutrophil and an eosinophil (南方医　图)

(2) Leukocytes: Move the specimen to observe different types of leukocytes.

1) Neutrophilic granulocytes (neutrophils): The leukocyte most commonly seen is neutrophil . They are spherical with larger size than erythorocytes. They can be recognized by darkly stained and rod-shaped or segmented nuclei consisting of two to five (usually three) lobes, each linked by fine threads of chromatin, and the presence of pink specific granules (more abundant) interspersed with fine purplish red azurophilic granules. Specific granules can be clearly distinguished from the azurophilic granules under immersion objective.

2) Eosinophils: Eosinophils are a little larger but far less common in the blood stream than neutrophils. The cell often contains a characteristic bi-lobed nucleus. The main feature of eosinophils is the presence of many coarse, large red eosinophilic granules evenly distributed in the cytoplasm.

3) Basophils: Basophils make up less than 1% of leukocytes and are therefore difficult to locate in blood smears. They have similar size to the neutrophils. The nucleus is S-shaped or irregular, and usually obscured by the overlying purplish blue basophilic granules of different sizes in the cytoplasm.

4) Monocytes: Monocytes are the largest leukocytes, being spherical or ovoid in shape. The nucleus is oval, horseshoe or kidney shaped. The delicate chromatin is

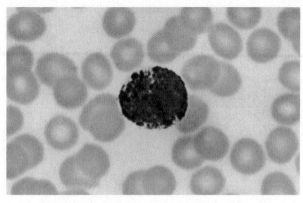

Fig. 4-3 A basophil (南方医　图)

less condensed and therefore stains lighter. The cytoplasm is gray-blue and frequently contains very fine purplish azurophilic granules.

5) Lymphocytes: Lymphocytes vary in sizes, of which small lymphocytes are predominant. The size of a small lymphocyte is similar to that of an erythrocyte. The small lymphocyte has a spherical nucleus, sometimes with an indentation on one side. Its chromatin is condensed and stained dark blue. The cytoplasm is scanty, appearing as a thin blue rim around the nucleus. The medium-sized lymphocytes are smaller than the neutrophils. The nucleus stains a little lighter, and the cytoplasm is more than the small lymphocyte. Small amounts of azurophilic granules are present in its cytoplasm.

(3) Blood platelets: Platelets are often present in clumps among other blood cells. A few individual platelets appear as irregular cytoplasmic fragments. Each platelet has a peripheral light blue stained

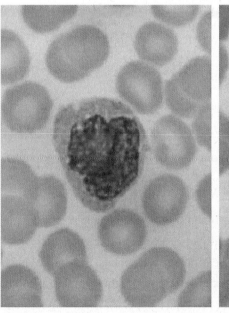
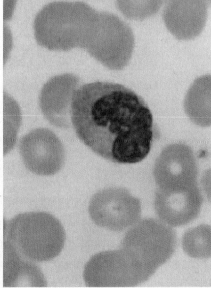

Fig. 4-4 Two monocytes (南方医　图)

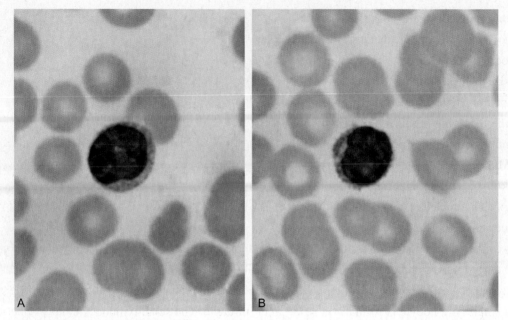

Fig. 4-5 Lymphocyte (南方医　图)
A. medium-sized lymphocyte. B. small lymphocyte

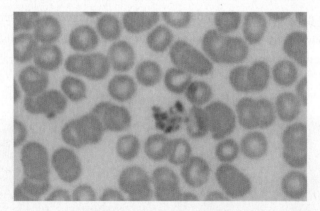

Fig. 4-6 A single platelet and a cluster of platelets (南方医　图)

transparent zone, the hyalomere, and a central zone containing purplish blue granules, called the granulomere.

Differential (leukocytes) count

Select any visual field except the periphery in the blood smear, and then identify and count each type of leukocytes in the field. Move the slide horizontally or vertically to change the fields. A total of one hundred leukocytes are counted and identified as neutrophils, eosinophils, basophils, lymphocytes and monocytes by the shape and appearance of the nucleus, the color of the cytoplasm, and the presence and the color of granules. The percentage of each cell type is reported according to their numbers.

(by Dong Weiren)

Chapter 5

Cartilage and Bone

1. Hyaline cartilage (trachea, TS)

Specimen No.____ Fig. 5-1

Preparation: HE stain

NE The blue stained C-form structure in the tracheal wall is hyaline cartilage.

LMag Observe the hyaline cartilage from the surface to the center.

(1) Perichondrium: Perichondrium is a thin layer of pink stained dense connective tissue covering the cartilage tissue.

(2) Cartilage tissue: Cartilage tissue is made up of a large amount of homogeneous cartilage matrix in blue-gray color; the chondrocytes located in the matrix are either single or in groups.

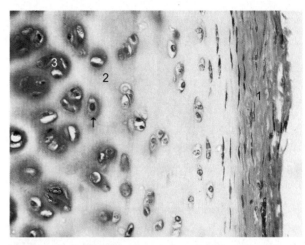

Fig. 5-1 Hyaline cartilage (trachea) (文建国　图)
1. perichondrium; 2. cartilage matrix; 3. isogenous group; ↑ cartilage cell and cartilage capsule

HMag

(1) Perichondrium: There are some darkly stained nuclei among the collagenous fibers. The cytoplasm is hard to differentiate from the collagen fibers. The cells in the shallow area are mainly fibroblasts, while the cells in the deep are mainly osteoprogenitor cells. These two kinds of cells have similar form and can not be differentiated.

(2) Chondrocyte: Chondrocytes vary in size and shape, and their form generally reflects the degree of maturation. At the periphery of hyaline cartilage, young chondrocytes are small and flattened, usually in single. In the center, the mature chondrocytes tend to be large and round or oval-shaped, they may appear in groups of 2 to 8 cells. These groups are called isogenous. The nuclei of mature chondrocytes are round and nucleoli are obvious, while the cytoplasms are weakly basophilic. Sometimes, a few vacuoles (lipid droplets) can be seen in the cytoplasm.

The cavities which the chondrocytes locate in are lacunae. The matrix surrounding each chondrocyte that shows more intense basophilia is the capsule or the territorial matrix. In sections, the cartilage cells are irregularly shaped and are detached from the capsule since they often shrink during the preparation.

2. Fibrocartilage (Intervertebral disk)

Specimen No._____ Fig. 5-2

Preparation: HE stain

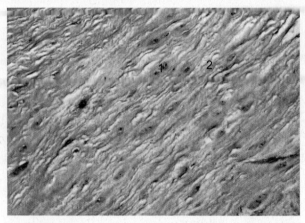

Fig. 5-2 Fibrous cartilage (intervertebral disk) (文建国 图)
1. chondrocyte; 2. collagenous fibers

NE The disk has two components; the central nucleus pulposus and the peripheral annulus fibrous. The latter is a fibrocartilage and is stained pink.

Microscope Fibrocartilage is characterized by numerous collagenous fibers and small amounts of ground substance. These collagenous fiber bundles surround the nucleus pulposus and are separated by chondrocytes in rows. Since it contains a large number of collagenous fibers, fibrocartilage is acidophilic and their lacunae are not obvious.

3. Elastic cartilage (auricle)

Specimen No._____ Fig. 5-3

Preparation: Elastic stain

NE The blue portion in the center is elastic cartilage, and the pink part at the periphery is the skin.

Microscope Elastic cartilage is essentially identical to hyaline cartilage except that it contains abundant fine elastic fibers in the ground substance. The fibers are stained blue.

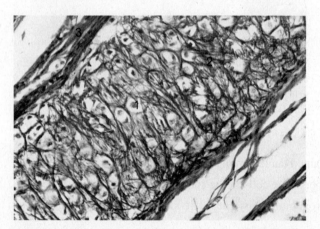

Fig. 5-3 Elastic cartilage (auricle, elastic stain) (南方医 图)
1. chondrocyte; 2. elastic fibers; 3. perichondrium

4. Compact bone (Diaphysis of long bone, TS & LS)

Specimen No._____ Fig. 5-4, Fig. 5-5

Preparation: Paraffin section or ground section, thiamine or Dahlia violet stain. (The tissues for paraffin embedding must be decalcified by acid solution in advance, for ground section the dried bone is used, therefore, some structures including perichondrium, blood vessels and cells, can not be kept well, even disappeared.)

NE There are two pieces of tissue on the slide. One is TS while the other one is LS. TS looks like a fan: the smooth convex is the external surface and the concave the internal surface.

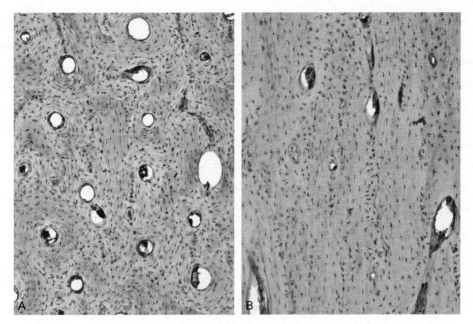

Fig. 5-4 Compact bone (diaphysis of long bone; thiamine stain) (文建国　图)
A. TS. B. LS

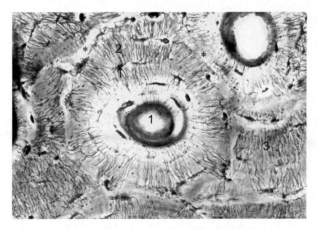

Fig. 5-5 Osteon (thiamine stain) (文建国　图)
1. central canal; 2. bone canaliculi; 3. interstitial lamellae; ↑ lacunae;
* cement line

LMag

TS

(1) Circumferential lamellae: There are several lamellae at both external and internal sides. The lamellae run parallel with the surface and in concentric circles around the axis of the bone. They are accordingly named outer and inner circumferential lamellae. Inner circumferential lamellae are located around the bone marrow cavity, and are thin and irregular. The thick outer circumferential lamellae are located immediately beneath the periosteum.

(2) Haversian system (osteon): Between the outer and the inner circumferential lamellae are many

round, oval or irregular Haversian system. It consists of a central canal (Haversian's canal) and some concentric Haversian lamellae surrounding the canal. At the outer edge of an osteon there is a thin layer of cement substance which appears as a refractory clear line (cement line).

(3) Interstitial lamellae: Interstitial lamellae are some irregular, parallel lamellae among osteons, or between the osteons and the circumferential lamellae.

In addition, some transverse or oblique Volkmann's canals can be seen. They are connected with the Haversian canals.

LS : The central canals appear as long slits. The lamellae are parallel to each other.

HMag Dark-appearing spaces among the lamellae are lacunae and canaliculi.

(1) Lacunae: There are a large number of small ovoid spaces (lacunae) between or in the lamellae.

(2) Canaliculi: They appear as thin and cylindrical lines extending radically from the lacunae.

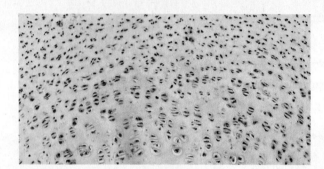

Fig. 5-6 Epiphyseal plate (LS) (文建国　图)
zone of resting cartilage

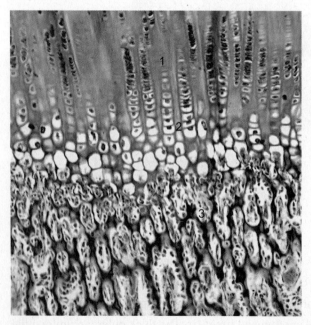

Fig. 5-7 Epiphyseal plate (LS) (南方医　图)
1. zone of proliferation; 2. zone of calcification; 3. zone of ossification; 4. transitional bone trabeculae

Canaliculi extending from the adjacent lacunae connect with each other and they also communicate with Haversian's canal. Generally, the peripheral canaliculi of an osteon do not cross the cement line, and they terminate here.

5. The development of long bone
(LS of decalcified fetal finger)
Specimen No.＿＿＿ Fig. 5-6～Fig. 5-8
Preparation: HE stain
NE The expanded end of the long section is epiphysis, and the narrow shaft with bone marrow cavity inside and bone collar at the two sides is diaphysis. The blue stained tissue between the two parts is the epiphyseal plate.
LMag Observe from the epiphyseal side to the diaphysis.
(1) Zone of resting cartilage: It consists of hyaline cartilage without morphologic changes in cells. Chondrocytes are small and scattered singularly in the matrix.
(2) Zone of proliferation: The larger and flattened chondrocytes form many isogenous groups which are arranged in longitudinal columns parallel to the long axis of the bone.

(3) Zone of calcification: The chondrocytes are round and hypertrophied. The cells close to bone marrow cavity appear degenerated and exhibit karyopyknosis, and their cytoplasm usually is vacuolated. Some cells are died, just leaving the empty lacunae in which the osteoclasts can be found. Cartilage matrix in this zone becomes calcified and dark-blue stained.

(4) Zone of ossification: This zone lies between the calcified zone and marrow cavity, showing interdigitation of red and blue. The chondrocytes have disappeared in this zone. The remnant of calcified cartilage matrix is covered by pink stained

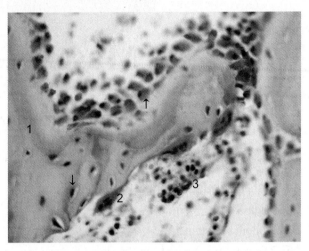

Fig. 5-8 Epiphyseal plate (zone of ossification) (南方医　图)
1. transitional bone trabeculae; 2. osteoclast; 3. bone marrow; ↑ osteoblast; ↓ osteocyte

osseous tissue with a layer of osteoblasts. These irregular cord-like structures are transitional bone trabeculae. The irregular spaces between the trabeculae are the primary marrow cavities which contain a number of immature and mature blood cells.

HMag Observe the ossification zone carefully. Osteocytes are embedded in the trabeculae. Pay attention to the morphological features of the osteoblasts and osteoclasts.

(1) Osteoblasts: Osteoblasts are located at the surface of newborn osseous tissue (the surface of bone collar and bone trabeculae) in a single layer. The cell is generally short columnar with a large round nucleus, and its cytoplasm is basophilic.

(2) Osteoclasts: Osteoclasts are often found in the lacunae in the zone of calcification and on the surfaces of transitional bone trabeculae. They are very large and irregular. Their cytoplasm is strongly acidophilic and each cell has several nuclei.

(by Wen Jianguo)

Chapter 6

Muscle Tissue

1. Skeletal muscle (limb, TS & LS)

Specimen No._____ Fig. 6-1

Preparation: HE stain

NE There are two sections on the slide, the long strip-shaped one is the LS and the elliptic one is the TS.

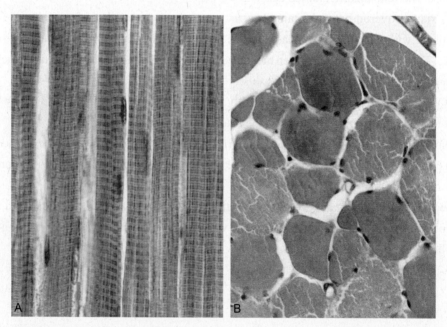

Fig. 6-1　Skeletal muscle (河北北方医　图)
A. LS. B. TS

TS

Observe the organization of skeletal muscle in particular.

LMag The connective tissue around the entire muscle is called epimysium. A muscle is made up of many bundles or fascicles of muscle fibers, which are variable in size. Each fascicle is surrounded by loose connective tissue termed perimysium. Each muscle fiber is surrounded by a small amount of connective tissue known as endomysium. There are blood vessels within the connective tissue. The muscle fibers in the sections appear round, elliptical or polyhedral, and the sarcoplasm is stained pink.

HMag One or several nuclei of muscle fibers, which are oblate, are distributed peripherally. Numerous dark red dots seen in the section are the cut ends of myofibrils. In the endomysial spaces, note the numerous capillaries recognizable by the eosinophilic erythrocytes contained within them. The wide endomysial spaces are a shrinkage artifact.

LS

Observe the structure of skeletal muscle fibers in particular.

LMag Skeletal muscle fibers appear as extremely elongated bands, being arranged in a parallel way. Between muscle fibers, there is delicate connective tissue (endomysium) which contains fibroblasts and capillaries.

HMag Each skeletal muscle fiber has multiple oblate nuclei located at the periphery immediately under the sarcolemma. On the thinner sections, myofibrils in abundance can be distinguished. They run parallel to the long axis of the muscle fiber and appear eosinophilic; but on the thicker sections, they are hard to distinguish. If the brightness of field is dimmed a little bit, the alternating dark- and light-staining cross-striations can be seen in each myofibril. The dark regions are called dark bands, and the light regions between the adjacent dark bands are referred as light bands. A dark line that bisects the light band is known as Z line.

2. Skeletal muscle (tongue)

Specimen No.＿＿ Fig. 6-2

Preparation: HE stain

NE A blue thin layer on the surface of one side of the section is stratified squamous epithelium. The red stained tissue beneath the epithelium is the skeletal muscle mainly.

LMag The longitudinally and transversely cut skeletal muscle fibers are arranged in a cross. The loose connective tissue surrounding each fascicle of muscle fibers is perimysium, which is variable in size. The

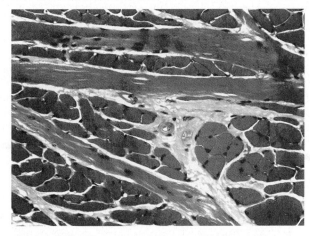

Fig. 6-2　Skeletal muscle of the tongue (南方医　图)

longitudinal sections of the muscle fibers, which are arranged in a parallel way, are elongated bands in shape, but the transverse sections of the muscle fibers are round, elliptical or polyhedral. The sarcoplasm is stained pink. Fibroblasts, fat cells and small blood vessels can be seen in the connective tissue.

HMag

(1) LS: Each muscle fiber contains multiple nuclei which are oblate and distributed peripherally. On the thinner sections, many myofibrils can be distinguished. They run parallel to the long axis of the muscle fiber and appear eosinophilic; but on the thicker sections, they are hard to distinguish. If the brightness of field is dimmed a little bit, the alternating dark- and light-staining cross-striations can be seen in each myofibril.

(2) TS: Each muscle fiber contains one or several nuclei which are oblate and distributed peripherally. In the sarcoplasm, some artificial cracks are often seen.

3. Cardiac muscle (LS of the heart wall)
Specimen No.____ Fig. 6-3, Fig. 6-4
Preparation; HE stain

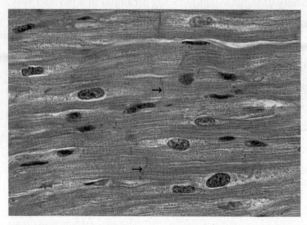

Fig. 6-3 Cardiac muscle (LS) (南方医 图)
→ intercalated disc

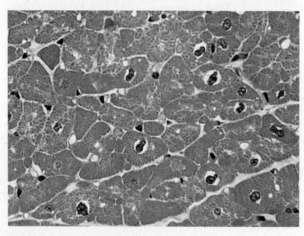

Fig. 6-4 Cardiac muscle (TS) (南方医 图)

NE The majority of red staining tissue is the cardiac muscle.

LMag The cardiac muscle fibers are red. Move the field to observe the various sections.

(1) TS: The cardiac muscle fibers are round or irregular in shape with variable size. A small amount of loose connective tissue and a lot of capillaries exist between the muscle fibers.

(2) LS: The fibers are short cylindrical and may branch to form network-like connections with adjacent fibers.

HMag

(1) TS: In some cardiac muscle fibers, a centrally located round nucleus can be seen, but in others, no nucleus can be found because it is not at the site of sectioning. The perinuclear cytoplasm stains light while the peripheral cytoplasm does deeper red.

(2) LS: The cardiac muscle fibers and their branches are linked end to end. Each fiber has 1 or 2 centrally located oval nuclei. The cytoplasm in the perinuclear region stains pale, occasionally containing brown-yellow lipofuscin pigment granules. The longitudinally arranged myofibrils also exhibit cross striations. At the sites of attachments between adjacent cardiac muscle cells, there are dark red transverse lines called intercalated disks, some of which extend across the fibers in a step-like pattern.

4. Cardiac muscle (LS of the heart wall)
Specimen No.____ Fig. 6-5
Preparation: Hemalum stain

LMag Find the longitudinal sections of the cardiac muscle fibers and then turn to high magnification.

HMag The dark bands of the cross striations are stained light blue and the intercalated disks dark blue.

5. Smooth muscle (jejunum)

Specimen No.____ Fig. 6-6

Preparation: HE stain

NE The red stained layer close to the smooth surface of the intestinal wall is the muscularis composed of smooth muscle.

LMag The muscularis can be divided into two layers, the longitudinal and the transverse.

HMag

(1) LS: The smooth muscle fibers are elongated, spindle-shaped cells that are closely arranged, roughly parallel to each other with the thickest part of a cell lying against the thin parts of the adjacent cells. Each smooth muscle fiber contains only one centrally located and darkly stained nucleus which is elongated rod-shaped or elongated ovoid, sometimes spiral-shaped. The sarcoplasm is stained red.

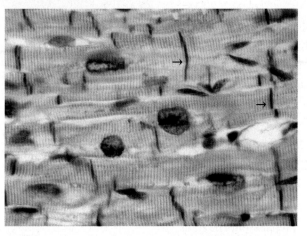

Fig. 6-5 Cardiac muscle (Hemalum stain) (南方医　图)
→ intercalated disc

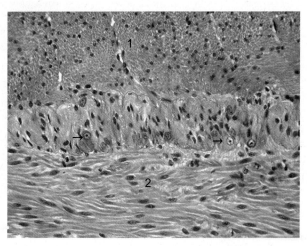

Fig. 6-6 Smooth muscle in the small intestine (邹仲之　图)
1. TS; 2. LS; → neuron of the myenteric plexus

(2) TS: The smooth muscle fibers are round or polyhedral. The nuclei can be seen only in the larger planes of the fibers.

(by Li He)

Chapter 7

Nervous Tissue

1. Neuron (spinal cord, TS)

Specimen No._____ Fig.7-1, Fig.7-2

Preparation: HE stain

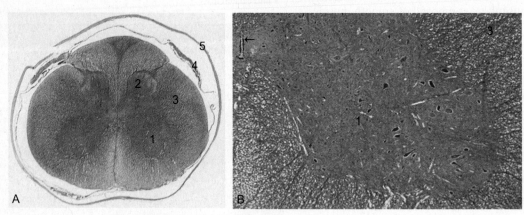

Fig. 7-1 Spinal cord (TS) (曾园山　图)

A. complete. B. part. 1. gray matter, anterior horn; 2. gray matter, posterior horn; 3. white matter; 4. pia mater and arachnoid; 5. dura mater; ← central canal

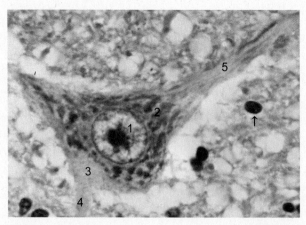

Fig. 7-2 Multipolar neuron of spinal cord (保天然、廖德阳　图)

1. nucleus; 2. Nissl body; 3 .axon hillock; 4. axon; 5. dendrite; ↑ nucleus of neuroglial cell

NE The TS of spinal cord appears round and is enveloped by spinal meninges. The peripheral area is white matter which is stained blue. The central butterfly-shaped area is gray matter which is stained purple. The gray matter has two thick anterior horns and two thin posterior horns. Put one anterior horn under the lens.

LMag In the anterior horn many multipolar neurons of different sizes can be found. Between the neurons are many small nuclei of the neuroglial cells, whose cytoplasm are unidentifiable. Choose big neurons for observation by high power lens.

HMag

(1) Cell body: It is large and irregularly shaped; the big and round nucleus locates in the center. Nuclear envelop is obvious and the euchromatin is plentiful and lightly stained. Nucleolus is also big and round. The cytoplasm contains many basophilic Nissl bodies. Nissl bodies appear plaque or granular with different sizes and are evenly distributed.

(2) Dendrite: One or more dendrites stretch out from the cell body and become thinner gradually. Nissl bodies can be observed in the dendrites.

(3) Axon: The axon arises from the axon hillock, an area of the cell body devoid of Nissl body, lightly stained and dome-shaped. The axon is thinner than the dendrite and contains no Nissl body. (Since each neuron has only one axon, for most cell bodies of neurons, their axons are seldom observed in the section.)

2. Neurofibril (spinal cord, TS)

Specimen No._____ Fig. 7-3

Preparation: Silver stain

LMag Choose a large multipolar neuron in the anterior horn, and observe it with high power lens.

HMag Neurofibril is brownish-black and filament-shaped. Many neurofibrils interlace to form a network in the cell body, but in the processes (dendrites and axon) they are parallel.

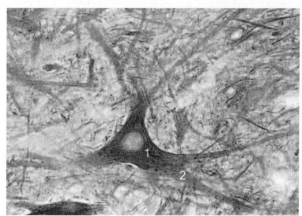

Fig. 7-3 Multipolar neuron of spinal cord (silver stain) (复旦上医 图)
1. neurofibrils; 2. process

3. Astrocyte (cerebrum)

Specimen No._____ Fig. 7-4

Preparation: silver stain

NE The section of cerebrum is stained yellow.

LMag

(1) Protoplasmic astrocyte: Protoplasmic astrocytes are distributed in the gray matter (the superficial area). The cell body is small and darkly stained. The processes are short and thick and have many branches.

(2) Fibrous astrocyte: Fibrous astrocytes are distributed in the white matter (the deep area). The cell body is small and darkly

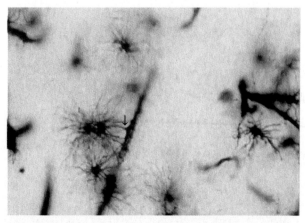

Fig. 7-4 Fibrous astrocytes in the cerebral cortex (silver stain) (复旦上医 图)
↓ the terminal of a process forms end foot sticking on the wall of a capillary

stained, too. Compared to those of the protoplasmic astrocytes, the processes of fibrous astrocytes are long and thin and have fewer branches.

HMag (Since the processes of astrocytes are located in different planes of the section, it is needed to use the fine adjustment to focus the image continually.) Some large, thin and flat processes' terminals stick on the walls of capillaries to form the end feet.

4. Nerve and nerve fiber (sciatic nerve, TS & LS)

Specimen No.＿＿ Fig. 7-5 ~ Fig. 7-7

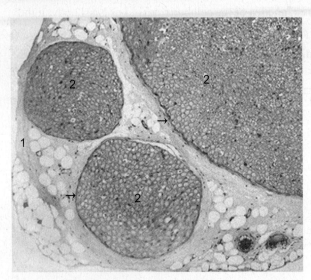

Fig. 7-5 Sciatic nerve (TS) (曾园山　图)
1 epineurium; 2 nerve fiber bundle; → perineurium

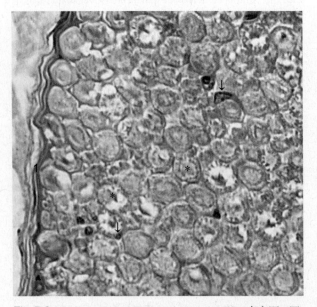

Fig. 7-6 Myelinated nerve fibers (sciatic nerve, TS) (南方医　图)
1. perineurium; * axon; ↓ the nucleus of Schwann cell

Preparation: HE stain

NE The TS of nerve is round-shaped and the LS is strip-shaped.

TS of nerve

LMag

(1) Epineurium: The epineurium is the connective tissue surrounding the nerve.

(2) Perineurium: There are many nerve fiber bundles (round and of different sizes) in the nerve. 1 ~ 2 layers of flat cells comprise the perineurium wrapping each nerve fiber bundle. There are some connective tissue, adipose tissue and blood vessels among the nerve fiber bundles.

(3) Endoneurium: The endoneurium is a layer of very thin connective tissue surrounding each never fiber in the nerve fiber bundle (observed properly with the high power lens).

HMag Myelinated nerve fibers show round shape and inequality of caliber.

(1) Axon: The axon is the round pink or grayish-blue spot located in the centre of each nerve fiber.

(2) Schwann cell: The Schwann cells surround each axon and have three parts.

1) Internal cytoplasm of Schwann cell envelops the axon tightly. It is a very thin pink layer.

2) Myelin sheath is a thick and circular layer of pink webs made up of protein,

because the lipid of the myelin sheath dissolved and disappeared during the preparation.

3) External cytoplasm of Schwann cells surrounds the myelin sheath. It is thin and pink stained, the half-moon-shaped nucleus can be found here in some cases.

LS of nerve

LMag Some nerve fiber bundles are arranged in parallel with inequality of caliber. There are some connective tissue, adipose tissue and blood vessels between nerve fiber bundles.

HMag

Myelinated nerve fiber

(1) Axon: The axon is located in the centre

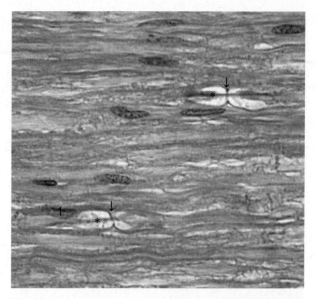

Fig. 7-7 Myelinated nerve fibers (sciatic nerve, LS) (南方医 图)
1. the nucleus of Schwann cell; * axon; ↓ Ranvier node

of every myelinated nerve fiber as a line, pink or grayish-blue.

(2) Schwann cell: The Schwann cells are located at the two sides of axon.

1) The myelin sheath appears as two thick layers of pink webs at the two sides of an axon respectively.

2) The Ranvier node is the constricted region between adjacent Schwann cells. They are discontinuities in the myelin sheath; the nerve fiber becomes thin here and appears like a cross.

3) The nucleus is a long rod-like structure and located in the scanty cytoplasm outside the myelin sheath at the middle segment of the cell.

Unmyelinated nerve fiber

It contains several red thin lines (axons) and run between myelinated nerve fibers. Oval nuclei of Schwann cells locate among these lines. The boundary of the fibers can not be distinguished.

The structures outside the nerve fibers constitute the endoneurium, containing some fibrocytes which have fusiform and darkly stained nuclei.

5. Motor end-plate (intercostal muscle or orbicularis oculi)

Specimen No._____ Fig. 7-8

Preparation: Stretched preparation and aurum chloride stain

Fig. 7-8 Motor end plate in the skeletal muscle (aurum chloride stain) (保天然、廖德阳 图)
1. motor end plate; 2. nerve fiber bundle

LMag Skeletal muscle fibers show pale hyacinthine, of which the cross-striations are clear. Nerve fibers are the black lines, and appear as fasciculation. The terminals of branches of each nerve fiber cohere to the superficial covering of the skeletal muscle fibers.

HMag The terminal of single nerve fiber expands as claw-like or botryoidalis, and cohere to superficial covering of muscle fiber. This structure is the motor end plate.

6. Meissner's corpuscle & Pacinian corpuscle (palmar skin of finger)

Specimen No._____ Fig. 7-9, Fig. 7-10

Preparation: HE stain

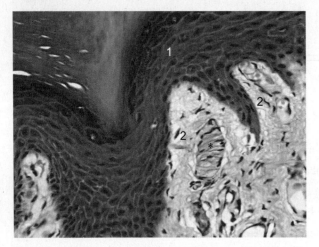

Fig. 7-9 Meissner's corpuscle in the finger skin (南方医 图)
1. epidermis; 2. dermal papillae; * Meissner's corpuscle

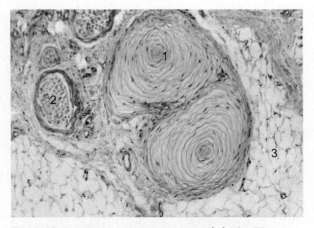

Fig. 7-10 Pacinian corpuscle in the skin (南方医 图)
1. Pacinian corpuscle (TS) ; 2. nerve fiber bundle; 3. subcutaneous adipose tissue

NE The darkly stained side of the section is the epidermis; the pale stained area is the dermis.

Meissner's corpuscle (tactile corpuscle)

LMag The connective tissue of the dermis protrudes into the epidermis to form dermal papillae. In some dermal papillae, the oval Meissner's corpuscles can be found.

HMag There are many flat cells arranged parallel in the Meissner's corpuscle. These cells have obvious nuclei. The Meissner's corpuscle is covered with a layer of thin connective tissue. With HE staining it is impossible to display the terminal of nerve fibers.

Pacinian corpuscle (lamellar corpuscle)

LMag It is located in deep dermis or subcutaneous adipose tissue, and appears big and round (TS) or oval (LS).

HMag Many layers of flat cells surround a core concentrically. The homogeneous core appears like a round spot (TS) or a bar (LS). With HE staining it is impossible to display nerve fibers ending in the core.

7. Meissner's corpuscle (palmar skin of finger)

Specimen No.＿＿＿ Fig. 7-11

Preparation: Silver stain

Microscope Meissner's corpuscles can be found in the dermal papillae. Some brownish-black nerve fiber endings wind among the flat cells which are lightly stained.

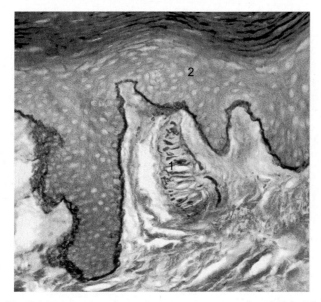

Fig. 7-11 Meissner's corpuscle in the skin (silver stain) (李海标 图)

1. Meissner's corpuscle; 2. epidermis

(by Zeng Yuanshan)

Chapter 8

Nervous System

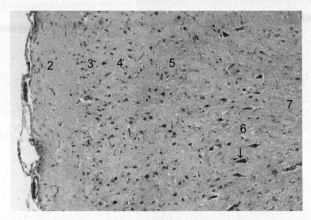

Fig. 8-1 Cerebral cortex (河北北方医　图)
1. pia mater; 2. molecular layer; 3. external granular layer; 4. external pyramidal layer; 5. internal granular layer; 6. internal pyramidal layer; (polymorphic layer is not prominent) 7. white matter; ↓ large pyramidal cell

1. Cerebrum (cerebral hemisphere)
Specimen No.____ Fig. 8-1
Preparation: HE stain
NE The depression of the cortical surface is sulcus, while the eminence is gyrus. The cortex (gray matter) is darkly stained while the medulla (white matter) is pale stained.

LMag
(1) Cerebral pia mater: It covers the cerebral cortex and is composed of a thin layer of connective tissue and some small blood vessels.

(2) Cortex: The neurons are arranged in layers. In HE stained section, the cell bodies and nuclei of neurons, the nuclei of neuroglial cells can be identified. The cerebral cortex exhibits six layers of neurons generally, but the boundaries between the layers are not very clear.

1) Molecular layer: It is the most superficial layer. The neurons are less, small and dispersed. This layer contains mainly horizontal cells and stellate cells.

2) External granular layer: It is thinner and contains much more neurons including many stellate cells and some small pyramidal cells which appear like pyramids.

3) External pyramidal layer: It is thicker and contains mainly medium-sized and small pyramidal neurons.

4) Internal granular layer: This layer is not obvious, containing some stellate cells and pyramidal cells.

5) Internal pyramidal layer: It mainly consists of some dispersed large and medium-sized pyramidal neurons.

6) Polymorphic layer: It is thick and contains fusiform cells and other neurons.

(3) Medulla: It is stained light pink. Some nerve fibers and nuclei of neuroglial cells can be observed.

HMag Choose a complete pyramidal cell to observe. The cell body is pyramidal shape and its round nucleus locates in the center of the cell body. From the top of the cell body an apical dendrite erupts and extends upward to the superficial layers of the cortex, but generally, only the basement of apical dendrite can be observed. The axon erupts from the bottom of the cell body (but it can not be found in all pyramidal cells because of the section).

2. Cerebellum

Specimen No._____ Fig. 8-2, Fig. 8-3

Preparation: HE stain

NE The cerebellar surface is deeply corrugated by transverse fissures and sulci that produce a series of deeply convoluted folds or folia. The area stained pink in the superficial layer of these folia and sulci is the molecular layer. Beneath it, the darkly stained area is the granular layer. The central red area of the folia is the medulla.

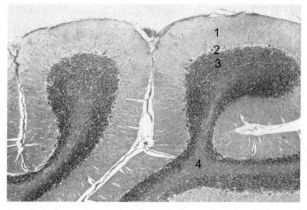

Fig. 8-2 Cerebellum (李海标　图)
1. molecular layer; 2. Purkinje cell layer; 3. granular layer; 4. white matter

LMag

(1) Meningina: It sticks tightly on the surface of cerebellum and inserts into the sulci. Meningina is a thin layer of connective tissue, including some small blood vessels.

(2) Cortex: It can be divided into three layers from superficial to deep.

1) Molecular layer: It is thick and contains less cell body of neurons; they are mainly stellate cells and basket cells.

2) Purkinje cell layer: This layer is the thinnest and composed of a layer of Purkinje cells bodies which are arranged regularly. The cell bodies are big and pear-like. The nuclei are

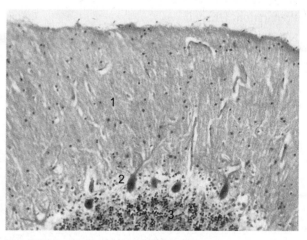

Fig. 8-3 Cerebellar cortex (李海标　图)
1. molecular layer; 2. Purkinje cell layer; 3. granular layer

big and round, and nucleoli are prominent. At the top of the each cell body 2～3 main dendrites erupt and extend to the molecular layer. The axon comes from the bottom of the cell body, but it can seldom be observed.

3) Granular layer: It is thick and densely packed with many small cell bodies of neurons.

(3) Medulla: The dispersed nuclei of neuroglial cells can be seen.

3. Spinal Cord (TS)

Specimen No.____ (see Fig. 7-1)

Preparation. HE stain

LMag Firstly to identify the white matter and grey matter, then identify anterior horn, posterior horn and lateral horn. Central canal of spinal cord locates in the center of the spinal cord. This channel has a lining of ependyma.

(1) White matter: It contains many transversely sectioned myelinated nerve fibers of different sizes and a few unmyelinated nerve fibers. The nuclei of neuroglial cells locate among the nerve fibers.

(2) Grey matter: It is composed of the cell bodies of multipolar neurons, nerve fibers and neuroglial cells.

1) Anterior horn: It is big and wide. Neurons here mostly are large and motor.

2) Lateral horn: Groups of small cell bodies of sympathetic neurons can be seen. (In some sections, the lateral horn is lack or not prominent.)

3) Posterior horn: It is long and thin, and contains less neurons. The neurons in the posterior horn are distributed diffusely.

4. Spinal ganglion

Specimen No.____ Fig. 8-4

Preparation: HE stain

NE The ellipsoid structure in the section is the spinal ganglion. In some sections, it can be found that the ganglion connects with a thin cord, which is the dorsal root of the spinal nerve.

LMag The surface of the ganglion is covered by the capsule which consists of dense connective tissue. The inner part contains groups of cell bodies of neurons (ganglion cells). There are some nerve fibers arranged parallel between the groups of neurons.

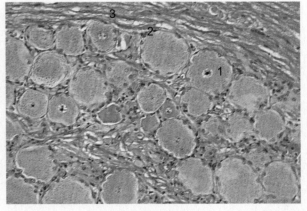

Fig. 8-4 Spinal ganglion (曾园山　图)
1. ganglion cell; 2. satellite cell; 3. nerve fibers

HMag

(1) Ganglion cells (cell bodies): They are mostly round and in different sizes. The big ones are stained light and the small ones are stained deep. The nuclei are round and centrally

located, the nucleolus is prominent. There are a lot of thin granular Nissl bodies in the cytoplasm.

(2) Satellite cells: Each ganglion cell is surrounded by a layer of satellite cells. They are flat or cuboidal. The nucleus is oval and stained light. The cytoplasm is not obvious.

(by Zeng Yuanshan)

Chapter 9

Eyes and Ears

1. Eyeballs (sagittal section)

Specimen No.____ Fig. 9-1 ~ Fig. 9-6

Preparation: HE stain

NE Recognize all parts of the eyeball referring the figures in this chapter.

Microscope Observe the wall of the eyeball from anterior to posterior and from outside to inside, and recognize the following structures one by one with LMag: fibrous layer (cornea, sclera), vascular layer (iris, ciliary body, choroid), and the nervous layer (retina). Then observe their details with HMag.

(1) Cornea

1) Corneal epithelium: The non-keratinized stratified squamous epithelium covers its external anterior surface.

2) Anterior limiting lamina: It is a transparent homogeneous thin layer in pink.

3) Corneal stroma: It is the thickest layer of cornea. It is mainly composed of many layers of collagen laminae which are parallel to the surface. Between them, there are some flattened fibroblasts.

4) Posterior limiting lamina: It is similar to the anterior limiting lamina but thinner.

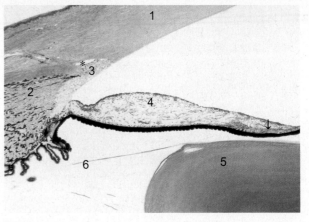

Fig. 9-1 The anterior of the eyeball (吉大白医　图)

1. cornea; 2. ciliary body; 3. trabecular meshwork; 4. iris; 5. lens; 6. ciliary zonule; * scleral venous sinus; ↓ sphincter pupillae muscle

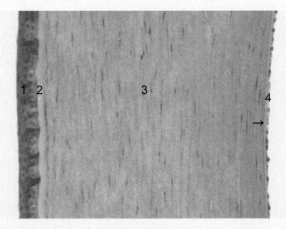

Fig. 9-2 Cornea (吉大白医　图)

1. corneal epithelium; 2. anterior limiting lamina; 3. corneal stroma; 4. corneal endothelium; → posterior limiting lamina

5) Corneal endothelium: It is simple squamous or cuboidal epithelium.

(2) Sclera: It is the outmost and the thickest coat of the five-sixths posterior eyeball and is composed of dense bundles of collagen fibers in regular arrangement. Anterior surface of sclera is covered by the bulbar conjunctiva which consists of loose connective tissue and stratified squamous epithelium containing melanocytes and goblet cells. At the transition zone from cornea to sclera, the sclera forms a slight protrusion called the scleral spur. The scleral spur provides a point of insertion for trabecular meshwork and part of the ciliary muscle.

(3) Corneal limbus: It is the transitional zone from the cornea to the sclera.

1) Scleral venous sinus (Schlemm's canal): It is located in the stromal layer of the limbus. The sinus is frequently present as an irregular shaped slit with endothelium lining.

2) Trabecular meshwork: It is adjacent to the inner side of Schlemm's canal and to the outer side of the anterior chamber angle. It is a pale stained, triangular and mesh-like structure and the trabeculae are covered by endothelium.

(4) Iris

1) Anterior border: The anterior surface of the iris is irregular and rough, with grooves and ridges. It is formed of a discontinuous layer of fibroblasts and pigment cells. Pigment cells are filled with pigment granules.

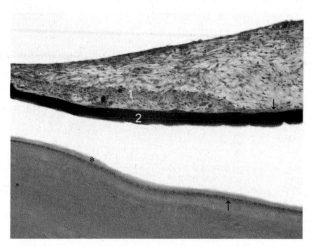

Fig. 9-3 Iris and lens (南方医　图)
1. sphincter pupillae muscle; 2. epithelium; * capsule of lens; ↓ dilator pupillae muscle; ↑ anterior epithelium

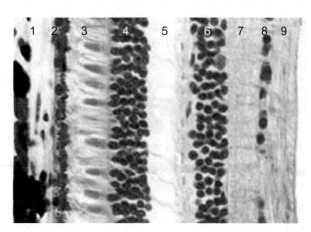

Fig. 9-4 Retina and choroid (马宁芳　图)
1. choroid; 2. pigment cell layer; 3. rods and cones; 4. out nuclear layer; 5. out plexiform layer; 6. inner nuclear layer; 7. inner plxiform layer; 8. ganglion cell layer; 9. optic nerve fiber layer

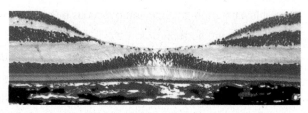

Fig. 9-5 Macula lutea and central fovea (复旦上医　图)

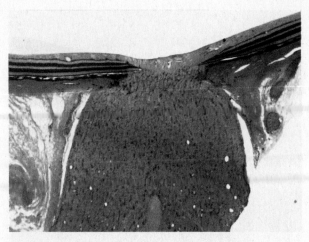

Fig. 9-6 Optic disc and optic nerve (复旦上医　图)

2) Iris stroma: It is thick and rich in blood vessels and pigment cells. Surrounding the pupillary margin, there is a bundle of smooth muscle, which is the sphincter pupillae muscle usually in transverse section.

3) Iris epithelium: Its anterior layer is composed of myoepithelial cells which are filled with pink stained myofilaments, creating the dilator pupillae muscle. The cells of the posterior layer are heavily pigmented with melanin granules.

(5) Ciliary body: It appears as a triangle. The ciliary processes are ridge like extensions of the ciliary body. There are silk-like ciliary zonules that connect the processes to the lens, but in section the zonules can not be seen clearly. From outside to inside the ciliary body is composed of three layers:

1) Ciliary muscle: They align in three directions: longitudinal, radial and circular. Between the muscular bundles there is a small amount of connective tissue containing pigment cells.

2) Stroma: It comprises a thin layer of loose connective tissue rich in blood vessels and pigment cells.

3) Ciliary epithelium: The inner surface of the ciliary body and its processes are lined by two layers of columnar cells, the outer cell layer is pigmented, whereas the inner cell layer is non-pigmented.

(6) Lens: The lens is a red biconvex structure. It has three principal components.

1) Lens capsule: It is a homogeneous and thin capsule.

2) Lens epithelium: It is a single layer of cuboidal epithelial cells that is present only at the anterior surface of the lens.

3) Lens Fiber: It is the main part of the lens parenchyma. The fibers appear as long, thin and flattened structures. The lens fibers at the periphery contain nuclei while those in the center have lost their nuclei.

(7) Choroid: It is loose connective tissue with abundant blood vessels and pigment cells. Its deepest layer is a thin hyaline homogeneous membrane called Bruch's membrane which separates the choroid from the retina.

(8) Retina: Eight layers from outside to inside can be identified.

1) Pigment cell layer: It is a layer of low columnar cells rich in melanin granules. The cell apex has abundant extensions that envelop the tips of the rods and cones.

2) Layer of rods and cones: It contains a large number of the outer roots of visual cells, the rods are thin and more, the cones are thick and less.

3) Out nuclear layer: It is composed of extremely dense nuclei of visual cells.

4) Out plexiform layer: It consists of the inner roots of visual cells and the dendrites from the inner nuclear layer.

5) Inner nuclear layer: A large number of nuclei aggregate in this layer but it is thinner than the outer nuclear layer. The kinds of the cells can not be recognized.

6) Inner plexiform layer: It consists of the axons from the inner nuclear layer, and the dendrites of ganglion cells.

7) Ganglion cell layer: The sparse but large nuclei of ganglion cells locate in this layer.

8) Optic nerve fiber layer: The axons of ganglion cells lie in this layer. Some small blood vessels can be seen. They are branches of the central artery or the central vein of the retina.

There are two special regions on the back wall of the eyeball in some sections: the papilla of optic nerve and the central fovea of the macula lutea.

2. Eyelid (sagittal section)

Specimen No._____ Fig. 9-7

Preparation: HE stain

NE This is the sagittal section of the human upper eyelid, it is thin and triangular in shape. The undulate side is the skin; the smooth side is conjunctiva. The tip edge between them is the margin of the lid.

LMag

(1) Skin: It is thin. At the eyelid margin there are some eyelashes, glands of Zeis (sebaceous glands) and sweat glands (Moll's glands).

(2) Subcutaneous tissue: Subcutaneous tissue is a thin layer of loose connective tissue.

(3) Muscle layer: It is skeletal muscle (the orbicularis oculi muscle), transversely sectioned.

(4) Tarsal plate: Tarsal plate consists of dense connective tissue and many branched tubuloalveolar glands called tarsal glands which arrange in parallel.

(5) Conjunctiva: The conjunctiva is covered by stratified columnar epithelium, and its lamina propria is a thin layer of loose connective tissue.

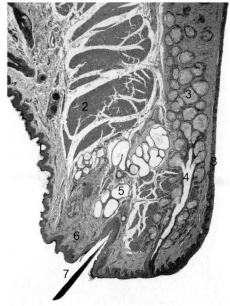

Fig. 9-7 Eyelid (sagittal section)（周国民　图）
1. skin; 2. orbicularis oculi muscle; 3. acini of tarsal gland; 4. duct of tarsal gland; 5. ciliary gland; 6. gland of Zeis; 7. eyelash; 8. palpebral conjunctiva

3. Inner ear (guinea pig)

Specimen No._____ Fig. 9-8 ～ Fig. 9-13

Preparation: The specimen was decalcified by acid solution in advance. Collodion embedding. HE stain.

NE The specimen is irregularly shaped, but the observer can find out a cone-shaped structure in it —— the cochlear modiolus, which is stained in scarlet red. Several sections of the cochlear duct are distributed in both sides of the modiolus. The other tissue around the cochlea is osseous tissue of temporal bone in which the sections of vestibule and/or semicircular ducts can be seen.

Cochlea, membranous cochlear duct and spiral organ

LMag

(1) Modiolus: The modiolus is the central conical bony pillar of the cochlea, composed of spongy bone in which the bone marrow, blood vessels and thick cochlear nerve can be seen. There are spiral ganglia in the lateral regions of the modiolus, close to the osseous spiral lamina extended by the modiolus.

(2) Osseous cochlear duct: Osseous cochlear duct is located at both sides of the modiolus; its cross section presents an oval shape. 6 ~ 7 transverse sections of the cochlear duct can be seen, because the spiral cochlea is coiled around the modiolus for about 3.5 turns in guinea pig.

Select a typical cochlear duct to observe. The triangular structure in the center of the cochlear duct is the membranous cochlear duct. Above the membranous cochlear duct is the scala vestibuli, beneath it is the scala tympani. Note the three parts of the wall of the membranous cochlear duct: a roof (vestibular membrane), an outer wall (stria vascularis and spiral ligament), and a floor (osseous spiral lamina and basement membrane).

HMag The basement membrane connects the osseous spiral lamina and the spiral ligament; there is a thin, dark red stained auditory string in it. On the basement membrane, there is a spiral organ

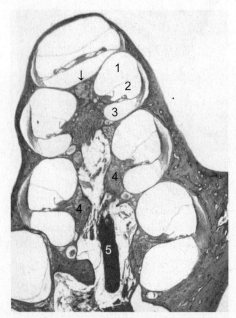

Fig. 9-8 Cochlea (pignea; LS) (南方医　图)
1. scala vestibuli; 2. membranous cochlear duct; 3. scala tympani; 4. spiral ganglion; 5. cochlear nerve; ↓ modiolus

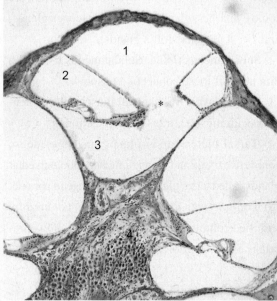

Fig. 9-9 Apical part of cochlea (pignea; LS) (田雪梅　图)
1. scala vestibuli; 2. membranous cochlear duct; 3. scala tympani; 4. modiolus; * helicotrema

(organ of Corti). Above the spiral organ, there is a pale pink tectorial membrane projecting from the top of the limbus spiralis. The tectorial membrane is often distorted because of the preparation.

Pay attention to the spiral organ.

(1) Supporting cells: They can be classified into pillar cells and phalangeal cells. Each kind can be subdivided into the inner and outer cells. The pillar cells have a broad base containing nuclei. The inner and the outer pillar cells connect each other at their bases and apices, so at the middle, they form a triangular tunnel (inner tunnel). An inner phalangeal cell locates at the inside of the inner pillar cell; while 3 to 4 outer phalangeal cells locate at the outside of the outer pillar cell. Above each phalangeal cell, there is a hair cell.

(2) Hair cells: The inner hair cell rests on the inner phalangeal cell; similarly, the outer hair cells rest on the outer phalangeal cells. The hair cell shows a columnar or flask shape, its nucleus is round and centrally located, and the eosinophilia of its cytoplasm is stronger than that of the phalangeal cells. Some static cilia can be seen at the top of some hair cells.

Semicircular canal, utricle and saccule (can not be seen in each section)

Microscope

(1) Semicircular canal and crista ampullaris: The TS of osseous semicircular canal presents a small round cavity in osseous tissue. The membra-

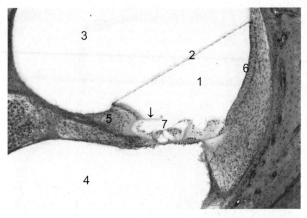

Fig. 9-10 Membranous cochlear duct and organ of Corti (文建国 图)
1. membranous cochlear duct; 2. vestibular membrane; 3. scala vestibuli; 4. scala tympani; 5. spiral limbus; 6. stria vascularis; 7. organ of Corti; ↓ tectorial membrane

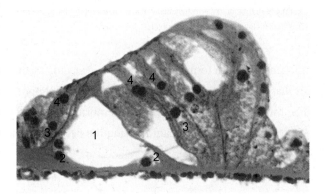

Fig. 9-11 Organ of Corti (复旦上医 图)
1. tunnel of Corti; 2. rod cell; 3. phalangeal cell; 4. hair cell

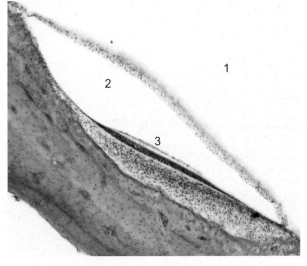

Fig. 9-12 Macula acustica (文建国 图)
1. vestibule; 2. saccule; 3. macula of saccule

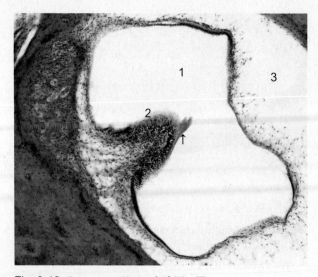

Fig. 9-13 Crista ampullaris (文建国　图)

1. ampullae of membranous semicircular canal; 2. crista ampullaris; 3. osseous semicircular canal; ↑ cupula (uncompletely preserved)

nous semicircular canal hangs on the wall of the cavity. The ampulla of each semicircular canal has an elongated ridge called crista ampullaris. Its surface is covered by a columnar epithelium and cupula which is a layer of pink homogeneous substance. In the epithelium, the nuclei at the base generally belong to supporting cells, and the nuclei in the middle belong to hair cells.

(2) Utricle, saccule and maculae acustica: The utricle and the saccule are similar in structure to the membranous semicircular canal, but their cavities are larger than the latter. The local thickened mucosa forms macula utricle or macula saccule. The basic structures of the maculae are similar to the crista ampullaris. They also have supporting cells and hair cells in the epithelium. The thin layer of colloid otolithic membrane covers the surface. The otolith can not be seen in section because it disappeared during the decalcification of the specimen.

(by Wen Jianguo)

Chapter 10

Circulatory System

1. Heart (LS)

Specimen No.____ Fig. 10-1 ~ Fig. 10-3

Preparation: HE stain

NE The thin portion is the wall of the atrium, the thick portion is the ventricle. Between them, the cardiac valve can be found pale stained and distorted, and this side is the inner surface (endocardium) of the cardiac cavity. Observe the structures of the atrium and ventricle from the endocardium towards the pericardium.

LMag

(1) Endocardium: The endocardium consists of a single layer of squamous endothelial cells resting on a thin sub-endothelial layer of loose connective tissue. Pale-staining Purkinje fibers can be seen beneath the subendothelial layer in the ventricle in some but not all sections.

(2) Myocardium: The myocardium is the thickest layer of heart wall. It consists of a large amount of cardiac muscle fiber bundles, few connective

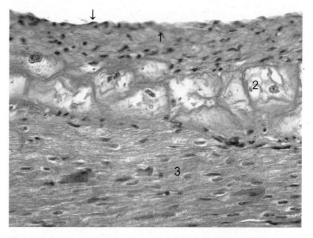

Fig. 10-1 Endocardium and myocardium (南方医 图)
1. subendothelial layer; 2. Purkinje fibers; 3. myocardium, cardiac muscular fibers (TS); ↓ endothelium

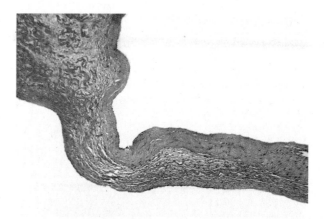

Fig. 10-2 Atrioventricular valve (南方医 图)

tissue and abundant small blood vessels. The cardiac muscle fiber bundles are oriented differently, so they are sectioned transversely, longitudinally or obliquely. The muscular layer of the ventricle is thicker than that of the atrium. The cardiac muscle fibers in the ventricle are also thicker than those in the atrium.

(3) Epicardium: The epicardium is thicker than the endocardium. It consists of simple

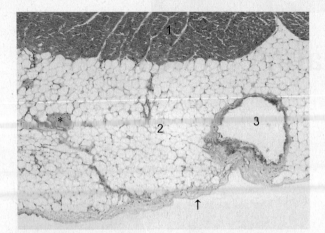

Fig. 10-3 Pericardium (南方医　图)
1. myocardium; 2. pericardium (adipose tissue); 3. small vein;
↑ mesothelium; * nerve

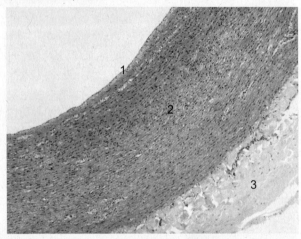

Fig. 10-4 Large artery (TS) (齐建国　图)
1. tunica intima; 2. tunica media; 3. tunica adventitia

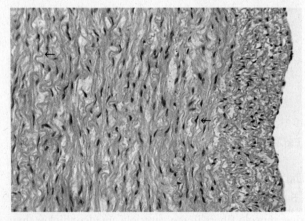

Fig. 10-5 Large artery (TS, part of the intima and media) (齐建国　图)
← elastic laminae

squamous epithelium (mesothelium) supported by loose connective tissue, and adipose tissue, small blood vessels and nerve fiber bundles can also be seen.

(4) The cardiac valves consist of dense connective tissue and endothelium on their surface.

HMag Purkinje fibers are considerably larger and irregular than ordinary cardiac muscle fibers. Each cell possesses one or two centrally located large nuclei, with an abundant, pale-staining cytoplasm and less myofibrils. Intercalated disks are seen between the adjacent cells.

2. Large arteries (TS)

Specimen No._____ Fig.10-4, Fig. 10-5

Preparation: HE stain

NE A portion of the wall of a large artery appears like an arch. The tunica intima is located at its concave side, and the tunica adventitia, which protrudes outward, is at its opposite side.

LMag

(1) Tunica intima: The tunica intima consists of endothelium resting on a subendothelial layer. An internal elastic lamina, although present, may not be easily discerned, because it is similar to the elastic laminae of the media.

(2) Tunica media: The tunica media is the thickest layer among the three layers of the artery wall. It consists of a series of concentrically arranged elastic laminae.

(3) Tunica adventitia: The tunica adventitia is thinner than the media. It consists of loose connective tissue and some small blood vessels (vasa vasorum).

HMag The media has 40~70 layers of elastic laminae arranged concentrically in parallel. The wave-like elastic laminae exhibit strong refraction of light, and are bright pink stained. Between the elastic laminae, the smooth muscle fibers can be seen.

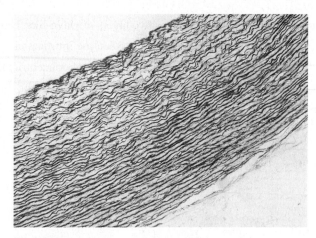

Fig. 10-6 Large artery (TS; Weigert's stain to show the elastic laminae) (齐建国　图)

3. Large arteries (TS)

Specimen No.____ Fig. 10-6

Preparation: Weigert's stain (special staining for elastic fiber)

NE The wall of the artery is stained generally in blue or blue-black.

LMag The media contains at least 40 layers of wave-like, blue or blue-black stained elastic laminae, between which are a few thin elastic fibers.

4. Medium-sized arteries and veins (TS)

There are also small arteries and veins, arterioles, venules and capillaries in this section.

Specimen No.____ Fig.10-7, Fig. 10-8

Preparation: HE stain

NE The structure with a thick wall and a round lumen is a medium-sized artery. The one with a thin wall and a larger, irregular lumen is a medium-sized vein.

LMag (HMag when needed)

(1) Medium-sized artery: The tunica intima consists of endothelium and

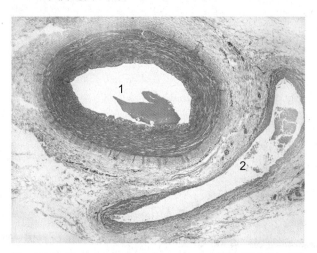

Fig. 10-7 Medium-sized arteries and veins (TS) (南方医　图)
1. artery; 2. vein

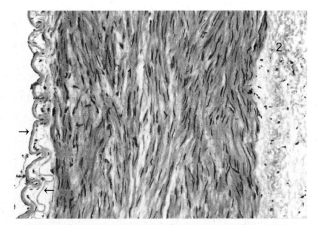

Fig. 10-8 Medium-sized artery (TS, part) (复旦上医　图)
1. tunica media; 2. external elastic laminae; → endothelium; ← internal elastic lamina

subendothelial layer. One or two layers of wave-like, bright pink stained internal elastic laminae are prominent and are located between the intima and the media.

The tunica media contains $10 \sim 40$ layers of concentrically arranged smooth muscle fibers, their nuclei are often twisted because of contraction of the muscle fibers.

The adventitia is similar in thickness to the media, and consists of external elastic lamina, loose connective tissue, etc. The pink stained external elastic lamina is thick and is composed of many discontinuous elastic laminae.

(2) Medium-sized vein: The intima is thinner than that of the medium-sized artery, and usually has a thin subendothelial layer, but this may be absent. The internal elastic lamina is not prominent. The media is thin and contains only several layers of smooth muscle fibers. The adventitia is thicker than the media. In some sections, some bundles of longitudinal smooth muscle (transversely sectioned) can be seen.

In the adventitia and the surrounding connective tissue, the small arteries and veins, arterioles, venules and capillaries can be observed. These structures can also be observed in the heart (Fig.10-9, Fig.10-10).

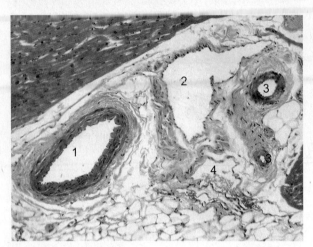

Fig. 10-9 Small blood vessels in heart (南方医　图)
1. small artery; 2. small vein; 3. arteriole; 4. venule

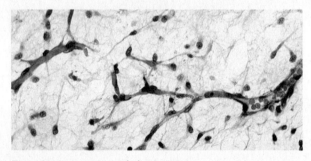

Fig. 10-10 Capilaries (南方医　图)

HMag

(1) Small arteries: The structure of small arteries are similar to that of medium-sized arteries. In the thicker small artery, internal elastic lamina attaches closely to the endothelium. The media is composed of several layers of smooth muscle fibers. The adventitia is similar in thickness to the media, and does not show a prominent boundary with the surrounding tissues.

(2) Small veins: Compared to the accompanying small arteries, the small veins have a thinner wall and a larger lumen. The media has one or two layers of smooth muscle fibers.

(3) Arterioles: Arterioles are smaller in diameter than the small arteries. The intima lacks internal elastic lamina. The media generally consists of one or two layers of smooth muscle fibers.

(4) Venules: It has a very thin wall and a larger, irregular lumen compared to the accompanying arterioles. Its wall consists of endothelium and connective tissue. A few scattered smooth muscle

fibers may be seen.

(5) Capillaries: It is the thinnest blood vessel, composed of a single layer of endothelial cells. However, most of the capillaries can not be identified in sections because their lumens collapse and in such cases their endothelial cells appear like fibrocytes. But a few capillaries with well preserved lumen can still be seen, especially those with red blood cells in the lumen.

5. Large veins (TS)

Specimen No.____ Fig.10-11

Preparation: HE stain

LMag (HMag when needed) The intima consists of endothelium and a few connective tissue elements which constitute the subendothelial layer. The media is thin, with a few layers of concentrically arranged smooth muscle fibers and some connective tissue. The adventitia is the thickest tunic, which consists of many longitudinal bundles of smooth muscle (transversely sectioned) and connective tissue.

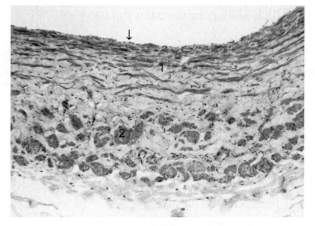

Fig. 10-11 Large veins (TS) (齐建国　图)
1. tunica media; 2. longitudinal bundles of smooth muscle in tunica adventitia; ↓ tunica intima (only endothelium)

(by Qi Jianguo)

Chapter 11

Skin

1. Thick skin (or hairless skin, from finger or toe)

Specimen No.____ Fig.11-1, Fig. 11-2

Preparation: HE stain

NE The epidermis comprises the cardinal red superficial portion and the blue deeper portion. The underlying pink layer is the dermis. The deepest and the lightest layer beneath the dermis refer to subcutaneous tissue.

LMag

(1) Epidermis: The epidermis is composed of keratinized stratified squamous epithelium. The cardinal red stained superficial part is stratum corneum, and the purplish blue part is the other layers of epidermis.

(2) Dermis: The boundary between the epidermis and the dermis is wavy. The dermis contains 2 layers with indistinct boundary — the shallow papillary layer and the deep reticular layer.

1) The papillae layer is thin, and consists of loose connective tissue with thin collagen fibers. The dermal papillae invaginate into the epidermis, tactile corpuscles and rich capillaries can be seen in them.

2) The reticular layer is thick and comprises dense connective tissue con-

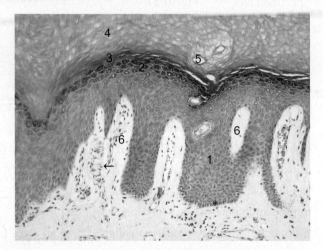

Fig. 11-1 Palm of the finger skin (周莉　图)

1. stratum spinosum; 2. stratum granulosum; 3. stratum lucidum; 4. stratum corneum; 5. spiral duct of sweat gland; 6. dermal papillae; * stratum basale; ← tactile corpuscle

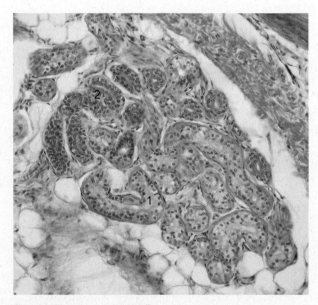

Fig. 11-2 Sweet gland (周莉　图)

1. secretory portion; 2. duct

taining many irregularly arranged and thick bundles of collagen fiber.

(3) Subcutaneous tissue: It consists of adipose tissue mainly, while the sweat glands, blood vessels, bundles of nerve fibers and lamellar corpuscles can be found in it. The boundary between the subcutaneous tissue and the reticular layer is poorly defined.

HMag

(1) Epidermis: From the base to the surface, five layers can be identified.

1) Stratum basale: It consists of a single layer of basal cells. They are columnar or cuboidal, basophilic cells resting at the dermal-epidermal junction. Some melanocytes can be observed between the cells in the stratum basale. They are round with pale stained cytoplasm and a darkly stained, oval nucleus.

2) Stratum spinosum: It consists of 4-10 layers of spinous cells. They are polygonal with round or ovoid nuclei and weakly basophilic cytoplasm. There are many small spines on the cell surface, and the spines of the adjacent cells form the mosaic. Some round Langerhans cells can be seen among the cells. Its cytoplasm is pale stained and nucleus is oval and dark.

3) Stratum granulosum: It consists of about 3 layers of fusiform cells. The cytoplasm is filled with basophilic keratohyalin granules, the nucleus is pale stained or disappeared.

4) Stratum lucidum: This is a thin layer of flattened, non-nucleated and eosinophilic cells without apparent cell profile.

5) Stratum corneum: It consists of many layers of flattened, non-nucleated and keratinized horny cells; the cytoplasm appears to be eosinophilic and homogeneous (filled with keratin). Some sections of the spiral ducts of sweat glands appear as a cluster of small lacunae through this stratum.

(2) Sweat gland: The secretory portion of sweat gland lies in the deeper dermis or subcutaneous tissue. It is composed of a layer of cone-shaped glandular cells with pale stained cytoplasm. Myoepithelial cells are observed beneath the base of the glandular cells. The duct of sweat gland is composed of 2 layers of small cuboidal cells, with weakly basophilic cytoplasm.

2. Scalp (or hairy skin)

Specimen No.＿＿＿ Fig.11-3, Fig. 11-4

Preparation: HE stain

NE The darkly stained side is epidermis. Some hair shafts can be seen on the surface. Some dark dots in the subcutaneous tissue are hair bulbs.

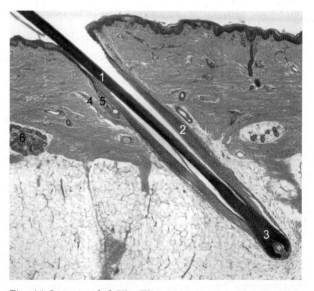

Fig. 11-3 Scalp (南方医　图)
1. hair root; 2. hair follicle; 3. hair bulb; 4. arrector pili muscle; 5. sebaceous gland; 6. sweat gland; * papilla

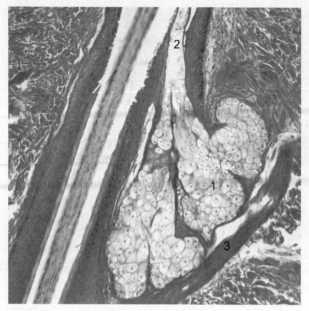

Fig. 11-4 Sebaceous gland (南方医　图)
1. acinus; 2. duct; 3. arrector pili muscle

LMag The histological structure of the scalp is similar to that of hairless skin, but the epidermis of the scalp is thin; only the stratum basale, stratum spinosum and stratum corneum can be identified generally. Many brown melanin granules in the basal cells are observed. Focus on the hairs and the sebaceous glands.

(1) Hair: The brown, long and wide bands are the hairs. They appear in LS, TS and oblique sections. The hair shafts are on the surface of the skin, hair roots in the hair follicle. A hair follicle comprises 2 parts, the inner epithelial root sheath and the outer connective tissue root sheath; the former is continuous with the epidermis, its structure being similar to it, while the latter is composed of dense connective tissue. The bases of the hair follicle and the hair root have a common terminal dilatation called the hair bulb. Hair matrix cells in the bulb lack apparent cell profile but are full of melanin granules. At the base of the hair bulb, a process of connective tissue and blood capillaries protrudes into it to form the papilla.

(2) Arrector pili muscle: It is a bundle of smooth muscle located between the hair follicle and epidermis, forming an obtuse angle. It can be found in some sections where one of its ends attaches to the hair follicle and the other to the epidermis.

(3) Sebaceous gland: It lies between the hair follicle and the arrector pili muscle. It is composed of one or several sac-like acini and a very short duct which opens into the upper portion of the hair follicle.

HMag At the periphery of an acinus in the sebaceous gland, there is a single layer of small cells with pale stained nuclei and weakly basophilic cytoplasm. In the center the cells are large; their nuclei are pyknotic and cytoplasm full of small vacuoles (lipid droplets that have dissolved during the preparation of the specimen).

3. Thin skin (or hairy skin, from the back or the abdomen)
Specimen No.____ Fig.11-5
Preparation: HE stain
Microscope The structure of thin skin is similar to that of the scalp, but comparing the latter, it has less hairs, shorter hair roots and follicles, less melanin granules in the hairs, poorly developed sebaceous glands and arrector pili muscles.

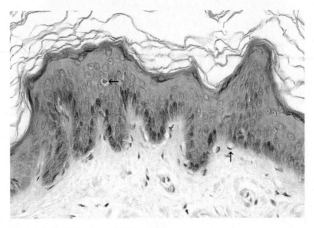

Fig. 11-5 Thin skin (周莉　图)
↑ melanocyte; ← Langerhans cell

(by Zhou Li)

Chapter 12

Immune System

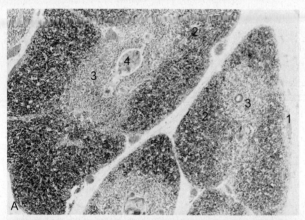

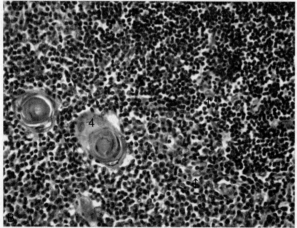

Fig. 12-1 Thymus (infant) (A. 河北北方医 B. 南方医 图)
A. LMag. B. HMag. 1. capsule; 2. cortex; 3. medulla; 4. Hassal's corpuscle; ↑ thymic epithelial cell

1. Thymus (infant)

Specimen No._____ Fig. 12-1

Preparation: HE stain

NE The thymus has a pink stained capsule on its surface. The parenchyma consists of lobules in various sizes. Each lobule contains an outer dark-blue cortex and a less basophilic central part, the medulla.

LMag

(1) Capsule: It is composed of a thin layer of connective tissue, which extends into the parenchyma and divides it into many incomplete lobules.

(2) Thymic lobules: Each lobule contains an outer dark-blue cortex, but the central pale medulla is continuous with those of the adjacent lobules. The pink stained thymic corpuscle (Hassall's corpuscle) is the characteristic component of the medulla.

HMag

(1) Cortex: It contains densely packed thymocytes and less numerous thymic epithelial cells. The small thymocytes are extremely basophilic due to the intensely stained nuclei. The thymic epithelial cells are scattered among the thymocytes; they are irregular in shape, with large, oval and pale nuclei.

(2) Medulla: The lymphocytes are less numerous than that in the cortex. Thymic corpuscles are isolated pink stained masses, various in size, and are composed of closely packed whorls of medullary epithelial cells, which become degenerated with shrank nuclei or are non-nucleated with intense eosinophilia.

2. Thymus (adult)

Specimen No. _____ Fig. 12-2

Preparation: HE stain

NE The thymus has no distinct lobular architecture and the parenchyma is dramatically atrophied.

LMag The small irregular areas of thymic tissue is surrounded by a mass of adipose tissue; both the cortex and medulla are thinner. A few thymic corpuscles can be found in the medulla.

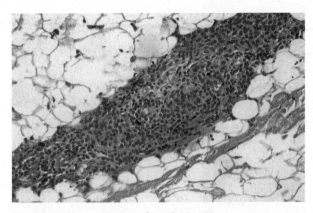

Fig. 12-2 Thymus (adult) (复旦上医　图)

3. Lymph node

Specimen No._____ Fig. 12-3 ~ Fig. 12-6

Preparation: HE stain

NE Lymph nodes are ovoid or bean-shaped with an indentation, the hilum, at the depressed side (it can not be seen in some sections). The pink tissue at the surface is the capsule. The dark blue tissue at the periphery of the parenchyma is the cortex, while the central light area is the medulla.

LMag

(1) Capsule and trabeculae: The capsule is made up of dense connective tissue surrounding the node. There are some afferent lymphatic vessels in it. At the hilum, the capsule is thick and extends into the node, in which blood vessels and efferent lymphatic vessels with wider lumen can be found. From the capsule and hilum, the connective tissue extends inward to form the trabeculae, which appears as pink and irregular.

(2) Cortex: The cortex forms the peripheral portion of the node, which is composed of an outer cortex, a paracortical zone and cortical sinuses.

1) Outer cortex: The outer cortex contains many lymphoid nodules and diffuses lymphoid tissue situated between the nodules. The secondary lymphoid nodules in the sections have various sizes, usually with pale stained germinal center (the dark zone and the light zone can be distinguished with the typical structures) and dark colored cap around it.

2) Paracortical zone: Paracortical zone

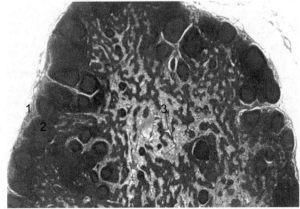

Fig. 12-3 Lymph node (复旦上医　图)

1. capsule; 2. cortex; 3. medulla

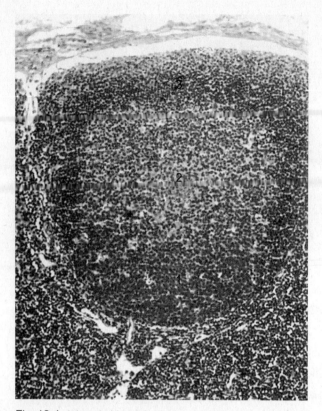

Fig. 12-4 A lymphoid nodule in the cortex of lymph node (复旦上医 图)

1. dark zone; 2. light zone; 3. cap

lies in the deeper region of the cortex, and consists of diffuse lymphoid tissue mainly. This portion has no clear boundary with the outer cortex and the medulla. The characteristic high endothelial venules (HEVs) can be found in this area.

3) Cortical sinuses: Cortical sinuses are situated beneath the capsule (subcapsular sinus) or surround the trabeculae (paratrabecular sinus).

(3) Medulla: The medulla is the central part of the node. It consists of the medullary cords and the medullary sinuses.

1) Medullary cords: The medullary cords are branched extensions of the inner cortex. They are irregular and stained in dark blue. In the cross section of the cords, blood vessels are usually found.

2) Medullary sinuses: The medullary cords are generally surrounded by medullary sinuses which are pale stained and have dilated lumen.

HMag

(1) Diffuse lymphoid tissue: Diffuse lymphoid tissue lies between the lymphoid nodules and is filled with small, round and basophilic lymphocytes. The reticular cells are scattered among the lymphocytes; they have pink stained cytoplasm, their nuclei are pale, irregular and with prominent nucleoli. The cytoplasm of the macrophages is strongly eosinophilic; their nuclei are small and dense. The interdigitating cells and reticular cells have similar morphology, so they can not be distinguished.

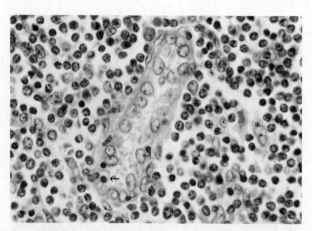

Fig. 12-5 High endothelial venule in paracortex of lymph node (傅俊贤 图)

← lymphocyte passing through the endothelium; * reticular cell

(2) Lymphoid nodules: The dark zones are usually small. The lymphocytes, densely aggregated

in this area, are larger with strongly basophilic cytoplasm. The light zone comprises less numerous medium-sized lymphocytes, macrophages and a few follicular dendritic cells. Both the dark zones and the light zones have supporting reticular cells. The darkly stained cap is formed by the numerous small lymphocytes.

(3) HEVs: Its endothelium is composed of cuboidal or columnar cells. The lymphocytes penetrating the endothelium can often be seen.

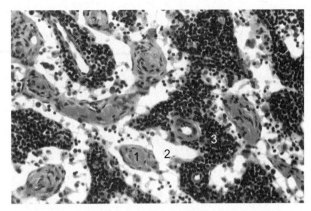

Fig. 12-6 Medulla of lymph node (复旦上医　图)
1. trabeculae; 2. medullary sinus; 3. medullary cord

(4) Lymphoid sinuses: They are spaces lined by squamous endothelial cells. In the lumen, there are stellate endothelial cells and macrophages which often send pseudopods (long cytoplasmic processes) to attach to the sinus wall.

4. Spleen

Specimen No.＿＿＿ Fig. 12-7～Fig. 12-9

Preparation: HE stain

NE One side of the specimen is covered with a layer of pink stained capsule. Most of the parenchyma in the section is the pink stained red pulp which is interspersed by blue stained white pulp.

LMag

(1) Capsule and trabeculae: The capsule is thick, and is invested by a layer of mesothelium. The dense connective tissue of the capsule extends into the parenchyma to form trabeculae which contain trabecular arteries, trabecular veins and smooth muscle cells as well.

(2) White pulp: The blue stained lym-

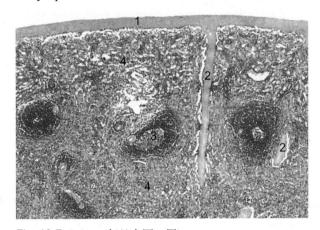

Fig. 12-7 Spleen (复旦上医　图)
1. capsule; 2. trabeculae; 3. white pulp; 4. red pulp

Fig. 12-8 White pulp of spleen (复旦上医　图)
1. lymphoid nodule; 2. central artery; 3. periarterial lymphatic sheath; 4. red pulp

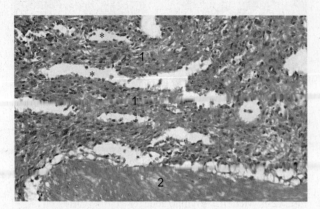

Fig. 12-9 Red pulp of spleen (南方医 图)
1. splenic cord; 2. trabeculae; * splenic sinusoid

phoid tissue distributed along the central arterioles forms the white pulp.

1) Periarterial lymphatic sheaths: They are diffuse lymphoid tissue surrounding the central arterioles, They present different shapes in TS and LS.

2) Lymphoid nodules (Malpighian bodies): They are located at one side of the periarterial lymphatic sheath, with its cap towards the red pulp. There is no clear boundary between the nodule and the periarterial lymphatic sheath.

3) Marginal zone: They are narrow transitional regions between the red and white pulps. They are filled with diffuse lymphoid tissue containing sparsely distributed lymphocytes. The blood sinuses in the marginal zone are called marginal sinuses.

(3) Red pulp: It consists of highly tortuous splenic sinuses separated by the splenic cords. They are stained red because of a large population of red blood cells.

1) Splenic sinuses: They are irregular tunnels, various in size, and occupied by different numbers of blood cells.

2) Splenic cords: They are irregular lymphoid tissue strands anastomosing to form the network rich in blood cells.

HMag

(1) Splenic sinuses: Find a splenic sinus without blood cells in the lumen. The rod-shaped endothelial cells are usually in transverse sections, with their round nuclei bulging into the lumen. Narrow slits can be found between the endothelial cells.

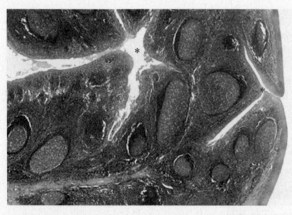

Fig. 12-10 Palatine tonsil (复旦上医 图)
* crypt

(2) Splenic cords: The red blood cells and the nucleated cells congregate to form the red and blue cell masses. The nucleated cells, such as lymphocytes, reticular cells, macrophages and plasma cells, usually can not be distinguished from each other.

5. Palatine tonsil

Specimen No.____ Fig. 12-10
Preparation: HE stain
NE One side of the specimen is the pharyngeal surface of the tonsil; the

blue stained portion is the epithelium. The dark portion beneath the epithelium is lymphoid tissue.

Microscope

(1) Epithelium: It is non-keratinized stratified squamous epithelium; which deeply invaginates the tonsil, forming blind-ended tonsillar crypts. This layer usually contains many intraepithelial lymphocytes.

(2) Lamina propria: It is beneath the epithelium and around the crypts, containing numerous lymphoid nodules and diffuse lymphoid tissue.

(3) Capsule: It is a layer of pink stained connective tissue in the deeper side of the lymphoid tissue.

(by Zhong Cuiping)

Chapter 13

Endocrine System

1. Thyroid gland

Specimen No._____ Fig. 13-1

Preparation: HE stain

NE In the section, many small, pink and round lumps are faintly seen, which are colloids of thyroid follicles.

LMag The capsule is thin and composed of loose connective tissue. In the parenchyma, plenty of follicles are present. The follicles have an extremely variable diameter, and are round or irregular in shape. The follicle is lined by a simple cuboidal epithelium and the cavity contains pink colloid. Outside each follicle, more or less connective tissue and small blood vessels can be seen.

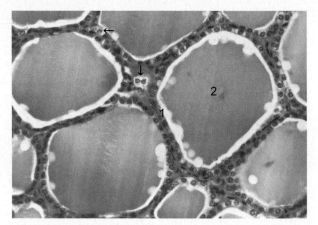

Fig. 13-1 Thyroid gland (吉大白医　图)
1. follicular epithelial cells; 2. colloid; ← ↓ parafollicular cells

HMag The follicular cells range from squamous to low columnar, generally cuboidal, with a round nucleus and pink cytoplasm. The morphology of thyroid follicles varies according to the functional activity. The follicles that are full of colloid and have a squamous epithelium are considered hypoactive; those contain a small quantity of colloid and have low columnar epithelium are hyperactive.

The parafollicular cell can be found singly or in clusters, as part of the follicular epithelium or as isolated clusters between the follicles. Parafollicular cells are larger than thyroid follicular cells, and are round or polygonal, with a larger, round nucleus and pale cytoplasm.

2. Parafollicular cells of thyroid gland

Specimen No._____ Fig. 13-2

Preparation: Silver stain

Microscope The parafollicular cell appears brownish-black stained with a light yellow nucleus,

58

while the follicular cells are stained yellow. The parafollicular cells are seen scattered between the follicular cells or as isolated clusters among the follicles.

3. Parathyroid gland

Specimen No._____ Fig. 13-3

Preparation: HE stain

NE A small parathyroid gland appears violet-blue stained.

LMag The parathyroid gland is covered by a thin capsule of connective tissue. In the parenchyma, the endocrine cells are arranged in cords or lumps; they may rarely form an isolated small follicle. A few connective tissue including some fat cells and capillaries can be seen in the gland.

HMag There are two types of endocrine cells. The chief cells dominate in number. They are small, polygonal cells with a round nucleus and pale cytoplasm. The oxyphil cells constitute a smaller population, distributed singly or in clusters. They are larger than the chief cells, and they are polygonal with a deeply stained nucleus. Their cytoplasm is strongly eosinophilic.

4. Adrenal gland

Specimen No._____ Fig. 13-4，Fig. 13-5

Preparation: HE stain

NE Adrenal gland appears as triangular or half-moon in shape. On the

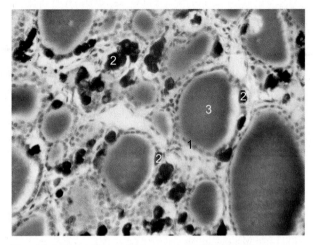

Fig. 13-2 Thyroid gland (silver stain) (齐建国 图)
1. follicular epithelial cells; 2. parafollicular cells; 3. colloid

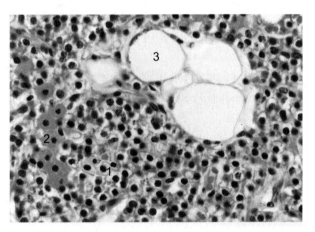

Fig. 13-3 Parathyroid gland (吉大白医 图)
1. chief cells; 2. oxyphil cells; 3. fat cell

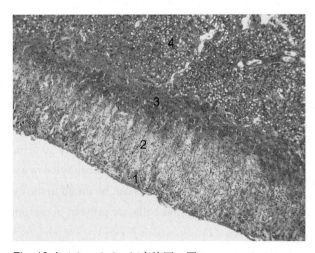

Fig. 13-4 Adrenal gland (齐建国 图)
1. zona glomerulosa; 2. zona fasciculata; 3. zona reticularis; 4. medulla

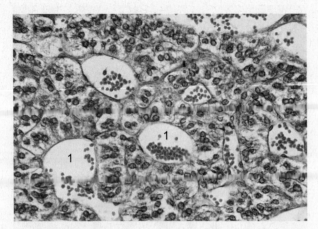

Fig. 13-5 Medulla of adrenal (齐建国   图)
1. sinusoid

surface, the light pink tissue is the capsule. The parenchyma is formed by two parts. The thick peripheral layer is the adrenal cortex, constituting most of the gland. The small and narrow central part is the medulla. The eosinophilic zona reticularis is a boundary between the two parts.

LMag

(1) Capsule: It is composed of connective tissue.

(2) Cortex: It can be subdivided into three concentric zones from outside inwards.

1) The zona glomerulosa is the thinnest of the three layers. The cells are arranged in round masses or arched cords.

2) The zona fasciculata is the broadest of the three layers. This layer is made up of the most pale-staining vacuolated cells arranged in one- or two-cell thick straight cords that run at right angles to the medulla.

3) The zona reticularis contains red stained cells disposed as irregular cords. The boundaries between the three zones and between the cortex and the medulla are not sharply defined, and the cell cords of the zona reticularis are often seen extending into the medulla.

(3) Medulla: The medullary cells are arranged in cords or clumps. Sinusoidal capillaries intervene between the adjacent cords. One or several sections of the central vein can be found, and its wall contains bundles of smooth muscle.

HMag Cells of the zona glomerulosa are small, pyramidal, with a small, deeply stained nucleus and weakly eosinophilic or basophilic cytoplasm.

Cells in the zona fasciculata are larger than those in the other two zones, and they are polygonal, with a large, round pale nucleus and pale staining cytoplasm containing a great number of vacuoles (lipid droplets).

Cells in the zona reticularis are small and polygonal, with a small, deep stained nucleus and strongly eosinophilic cytoplasm.

The medullary cells are polygonal and vary in size, with a round nucleus and pale stained cytoplasm. In adrenal glands that have been fixed in a solution containing potassium dichromate, many yellowish-brown granules can be found in the cytoplasm of the cells (chromaffin cells). A few sympathetic ganglion cells are present occasionally, scattered between the cell cords or clumps.

5. Hypophysis (Sagittal Section)

Specimen No.____ Fig. 13-6~Fig. 13-8

Preparation: HE stain

NE The hypophysis is oval generally. In one side of the section, the pars nervosa is seen as pale stained. In the opposite side, the pars distalis is deep stained, forming the greater part of the gland. The pars intermedia is located between the above mentioned parts.

LMag A thin connective tissue capsule covers the gland.

(1) Pars distalis: The glandular cells form many cords and a few small follicles are interspersed with numerous sinusoidal capillaries.

(2) Pars intermedia: It is a narrow region made up of follicles varying in size and filled with red or grayish-blue colloid.

(3) Pars nervosa: It is pale stained generally, composed of many nerve fibers, some cells and sinusoidal capillaries.

HMag

(1) Pars distalis: The acidophilic cells are more; they are large, round or oval, with a round nucleus and strongly acidophilic cytoplasm. Less basophilic cells are large, oval or polygonal, with a round nucleus and deeply basophilic cytoplasm. Chromophobes are smaller than the chromophils, they have round nuclei and faintly stained cytoplasm, without sharp boundaries with the neigh-

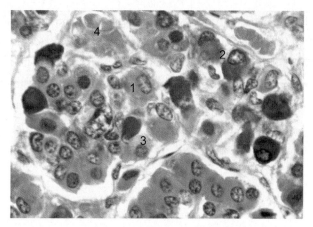

Fig. 13-6 Pars distalis of hypophysis (南方医　图)
1. acidophilic cell; 2. basophilic cell; 3. chromophobe; 4. sinusoid

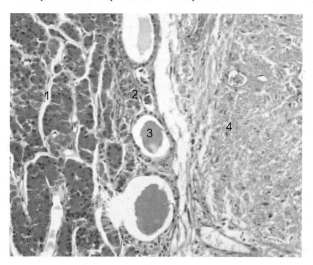

Fig. 13-7 Pars intermedia of hypophysis (南方医　图)
1. pars distalis; 2. pars intermedia; 3. follicle; 4. pars nervosa

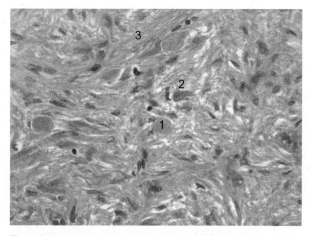

Fig. 13-8 Pars nervosa of hypophysis (南方医　图)
1. Herring body; 2. pituicyte; 3. unmyelinated nerve fiber

boring cells. Chromophobes are numerous and distributed singly or in clusters.

(2) Pars nervosa: It consists mainly of unmyelinated nerve fibers and pituicytes. The sinusoidal capillaries intervene between the fibers and the cells. The pituicytes are highly variable in size and shape. In addition, pink or occasionally grayish-blue stained rounded clumps, the Herring bodies, which are homogeneous and variable in diameter, can be seen.

(by Qi Jianguo)

Chapter 14

Digestive Tract

1. Tongue (perpendicular section)

Specimen No._____ Fig. 14-1 ~ Fig. 14-3

Preparation: HE stain

NE The rough and the blue stained side is the mucosa of the dorsal surface; the stained red tissue is muscle.

LMag Identify the mucosa and the striated muscle. The mucosa is composed of stratified squamous epithelium and lamina propria, including many lingual papillae.

(1) Filiform papillae: They appear conical in shape, being numerous and present over the entire dorsal surface. The superficial cells of the epithelium are often keratinized and appear red. In the axes of papillae is connective tissue of the lamina propria.

(2) Fungiform papillae: They are less numerous and are scattered among the filiform papillae. They are bigger and mushroom like, with a narrow stalk and a smooth-surfaced, dilated upper part. The epithelium does not keratinize and may contain taste buds. The axes contain rich capillaries.

(3) Circumvallate papillae: Since there are only 7-12 circumvallate papillae and they are located in the "V" region in the posterior portion of the tongue, they can not be found in each section. They are the biggest papillae with wider and more flattened upper

Fig. 14-1 Tongue (复旦上医　图)
1. filiform papillae; 2. fungiform papillae

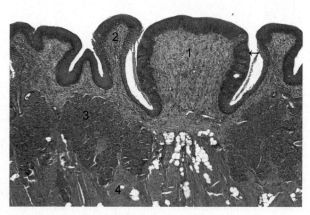

Fig. 14-2 Tongue (邹仲之　图)
1. circumvallate papillae; 2. fungiform papillae; 3. serous gland;
4. striated muscle; ← taste bud

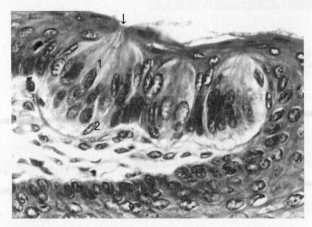

Fig. 14-3 Taste bud (河北北方医 图)
1. receptor cell; 2. basal cell; ↓ gustatory pore

surfaces. There are taste buds in their lateral epithelium and grooves beside it. In the lamina propria around the bottom of the grooves, serous glands can be seen.

HMag The taste buds are lightly stained ovoid corpuscles. In the upper part is a narrow taste pore towards the oral cavity. Two kinds of cells can be identified. The long fusiform taste cells (or receptor cells) have microvilli on the free surfaces, and the basal cells are located in the deeper part with small nuclei.

2. Esophagus (TS)

Specimen No. _____ Fig. 14-4

Preparation: HE stain

Preparation: HE stain

NE The lumen is irregular in shape because of existence of the folds (or rugae). Around the lumen, the stained blue layer is the epithelium. The pink tissue beneath the epithelium is mainly the submucosa, and the red tissue is the muscle layer.

LMag

(1) Mucosa: The epithelium is stratified squamous. In the connective tissue of the lamina propria, lymphoid tissue, small blood vessels and ducts of esophageal glands can be seen. If the specimen is from the region near the stomach, the mucous esophageal cardiac glands can be found. The

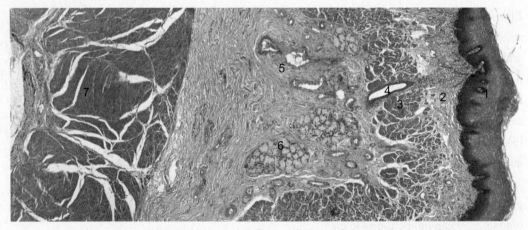

Fig. 14-4 Esophagus (TS) (邹仲之 图)
1. epithelium; 2. lamina propria; 3. duct of esophageal gland; 4. muscularis mucosae; 5. submucosa; 6. acini of esophageal gland; 7. muscle layer (inner circular layer)

muscularis mucosae are composed of many small bundles of smooth muscle fibers which are transversely sectioned.

(2) Submucosa: It is composed of loose connective tissue mainly, containing some groups of mucous acini of esophageal glands.

(3) Muscle layer: It is the thickest layer including an inner circular layer (being longitudinally sectioned) and an outer longitudinal layer (being transversally sectioned). The myenteric nerve plexus can be seen between them. Note that the type of muscle in different segments of esophagus is different.

(4) Fibrosa: It is composed mainly of loose connective tissue.

3. Stomach (the body or fundus)

Specimen No. _____ Fig. 14-5 ~ Fig. 14-7

Preparation: HE stain

NE The rough and blue stained side is the mucosa; there are folds at this side. The thick and red tissue is the muscle layer. Between them, the pink tissue is the submucosa.

LMag

(1) Mucosa

1) Epithelium is simple columnar, made up of surface mucous cells. The nuclei are ovoid at the base of the cells, the apical cytoplasm is lightly stained, and it even appears translucent because of the presence of many mucinogen granules. The epithelium evaginates into the lamina propria to form gastric pits.

2) Lamina propria is full of fundic glands which are in longitudinal, oblique or tangential sections. It can be seen that some glands' lumen open in the pits. There are a few connective tissue and smooth muscle fibers among the pits and the glands.

3) Muscularis mucosae is very thin and composed of smooth muscle.

(2) Submucosa: It is made up of loose connective tissue including arterioles, venules and lymphatic vessels. The submucosal nerve plexus can be seen occasionally. The submucosa and

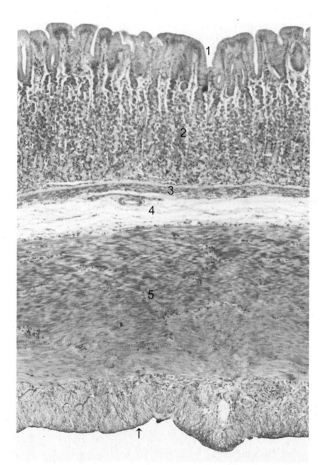

Fig. 14-5 Fundus of the stomach (河北北方医　图)
1. gastric pit; 2. fundic glands; 3. muscularis mucosae; 4. submucosa;
5. muscularis externa; ↑ serosa

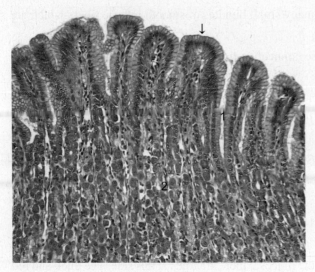

Fig. 14-6 Mucosa in the fundus (邹仲之　图)
1. gastric pit; 2. lamina propria (fundic glands); ↓ surface mucous cells

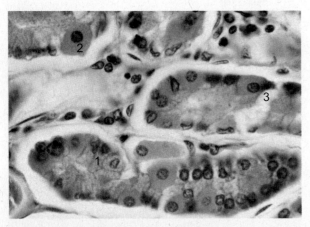

Fig. 14-7 Fundic glands (南方医　图)
1. chief cells; 2. parietal cell; 3. mucous neck cell

mucosa protrude to the cavity of stomach to form folds at some areas of the wall, and the submucosa is quite thick here.

(3) Muscle layer: The muscle layer of the stomach is very thick. It is composed of inner oblique, middle circular and outer longitudinal layers of smooth muscle, but the boundaries among them are not clear. The myenteric nerve plexus can be identified.

(4) Serosa: It is composed of thin layer of connective tissue and mesothelium.

HMag

(1) Parietal cells: They are mostly found in the upper part of the fundic glands. Parietal cells are mostly large and round cells. The round and darkly stained nuclei are seen in the center of the cells, in some cells there are two nuclei. The cytoplasm is eosinophilic appearing red.

(2) Chief cells: They are the most numerous and are distributed in the lower part of the glands mainly. These columnar cells are small, with round nuclei located in the base. The basal cytoplasm is basophilic appearing blue; in the apical cytoplasm some purplish-red pepsinogen granules can be found (but in most cases the granules have disappeared and this area appears light).

(3) Mucous neck cells: There are only a few of these cells distributed in the neck or in the upper area of the glands. The cells are small and appear like wedge between parietal cells. Their small nuclei are present in the base. The cytoplasm is lightly stained because of many mucinogen granules.

4. Stomach (pylorus)

Specimen No. _____ Fig. 14-8
Preparation: HE stain

NE It appears like the fundus except that the surface of mucosa is relatively flat.

LMag The structure of the pylorus is similar to that of the fundus, but the gastric pits are very deep, the pyloric glands are composed of mucous cells (in some glands in the area near the fundus, a few parietal cells can be seen).

5. Duodenum (TS or LS)

Specimen No. _____ Fig. 14-9 ~ Fig. 14-11

Preparation: HE stain

NE The luminal side is rough with some folds, many tiny processes (villi) can be seen on the folds, and the blue surface is the mucosa.

LMag

(1) Mucosa: On the surface there are many villi in longitudinal, transverse, oblique or tangential sections. The lamina propria contains many intestinal glands and occasional solitary lymphoid nodules. The muscularis mucosae is thin.

(2) Submucosa: In some regions, groups of mucous acini of the duodenal glands can be seen in the connective tissue; a few acini penetrate the muscularis mucosae and reach the deep area of the mucosa.

(3) Muscle layer: It is composed of inner circular and outer longitudinal layer of smooth muscle. The myenteric nerve plexus is prominent (Fig.6-6).

(4) Adventitia: It can be serosa or fibrosa.

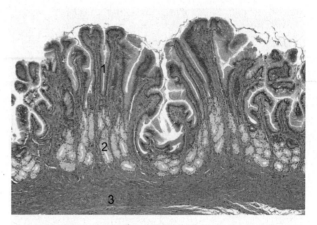

Fig. 14-8 Pylorus of stomach (邹仲之 图)
1. gastric pit; 2. pyloric gland; 3. muscularis mucosae

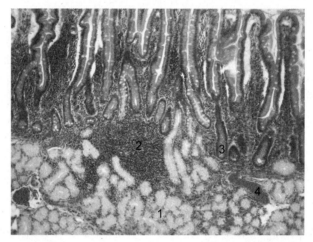

Fig. 14-9 Mucosa and submucosa in duodenum (邹仲之 图)
1. acini of Brunner's glands; 2. lymphoid tissue; 3. small intestinal gland; 4. venule

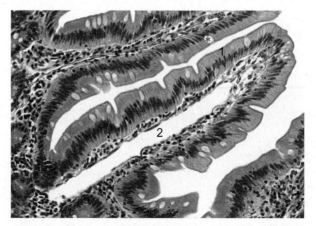

Fig. 14-10 Intestinal villus (李和 图)
1. absorptive cells; 2. central lacteal; * goblet cell

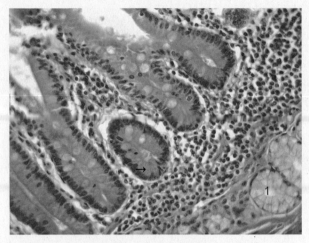

Fig. 14-11 Small intestinal glands (田雪梅 图)
1. acini of Brunner's glands; → Paneth cells

HMag
(1)Villi: The epithelium is simple columnar, single goblet cell scattered among many resorptive cells. The resorptive cells are high columnar with ovoid nuclei in the base. On the free surface, a red thin layer of striated border can be seen. The axes of villi are connective tissue containing some scattered smooth muscle fibers and a central lacteal. The wall of the lacteal is only a layer of endothelium, the lumen is relatively big. (But in most cases, the lumen is collapsed, so the lacteal is difficult to identify.)

(2) Intestinal glands: It is made of simple columnar epithelium; there are more resorptive cells and less goblet cell. At the base of the gland, there is a cluster of Paneth cells. They are pyramidal with basal nuclei and big eosinophilic granules in the apical cytoplasm.

6. Jejunum (TS or LS)

Specimen No. _____ Fig. 14-12

Preparation: HE stain

NE It is similar to the duodenum but the wall is thinner.

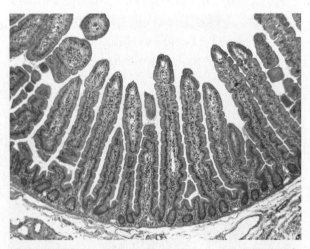

Fig. 14-12 Mucosa of the jejunum (showing plenty of intestinal villi) (邹仲之 图)

LMag The structure of the jejunum is similar to that of the duodenum, but the villi are thinner than those in duodenum and appear like fingers; there are more goblet cells in the epithelium. No gland can be found in the submucosa. The adventitia is serosa.

7. Ileum (TS or LS)

Specimen No. _____ Fig. 14-13

Preparation: HE stain

NE It is similar to the jejunum generally but some stained blue areas can be seen in the wall.

LMag The villi are short and pyramid like. There are more goblet cells in the epithelium. Rich lymphoid tissue including aggregated lymphoid nodules can be seen in the lamina propria, which often penetrate the muscularis mucosae and extend into the submucosa.

8. Colon (TS or LS)

Specimen No. _____ Fig. 14-14, Fig. 14-15

Preparation: HE stain

NE The mucosal surface is smooth. In TS, the eminence (taenia coli) can be seen at the serosal surface.

LMag Identify the four layers of the colon and compare them with those of the small intestine. The colon has the following characteristics: the mucosal surface is smooth without villus; the intestinal glands are densely packed with abundant goblet cells but no Paneth cell; solitary lymphoid nodules can be seen in the lamina propria; in the serosa there are aggregates of adipocytes (appendices epiploicae). In the TS of colon, in the outer longitudinal muscle layer, the congregate of muscle fibers (taenia coli) can be found.

9. Appendix (TS)

Specimen No. _____ Fig. 14-16

Preparation: HE stain

NE The lumen is very small, and many blue clusters (lymphoid nodules) surround it. Outwards, the pink area is the submucosa; the red structure is the muscle layer.

LMag To identify the four layers and note the characteristics: there is no villus; the intestinal glands are less and shorter; abundant lymphoid nodules and diffuse lymphoid tissue are located in the lamina propria and ex-

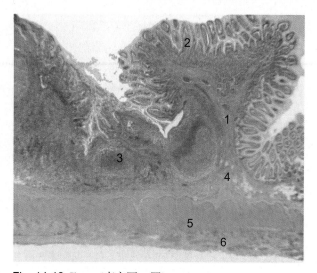

Fig. 14-13 Ileum (南方医　图)

1. fold; 2. mucosa (villi); 3. lymphoid tissue; 4. submucosa; 5. muscle layer; 6. adventitia

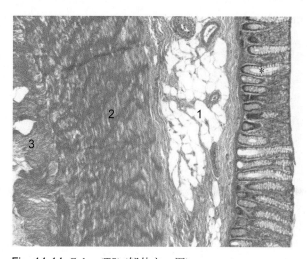

Fig. 14-14 Colon (TS) (邹仲之　图)

1. submucosa; 2. inner circular muscle layer; 3. outer longitudinal muscle layer; * intestinal gland

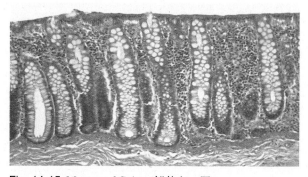

Fig. 14-15 Mucosa of Colon (邹仲之　图)

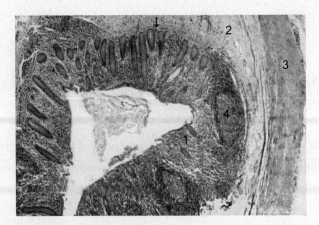

Fig. 14-16 Appendix (南方医　图)
1. mucosa; 2. submucosa; 3. muscle layer; 4. lymphoid nodule;
↓ muscularis mucosae

tend into the submucosa, thus the muscularis mucosae is far from complete; the muscle layer is thin; the serosa is continuous with the mesoenteriolum in some specimens.

(by Zou Zhongzhi)

Chapter 15

Digestive glands

1. Parotid gland

Specimen No. _____ Fig. 15-1

Preparation: HE stain

NE A parotid gland is covered with a thin layer of pink stained capsule; the inner blue stained masses are lobules.

Microscope The capsule is made up of connective tissue; the parenchyma is divided by pale stained connective tissue into many lobules which are filled with serous acini and ducts in different sections.

1) The intercalated ducts are continuous with the acini. They have narrow lumen lined by simple squamous or cuboidal epithelial cells.

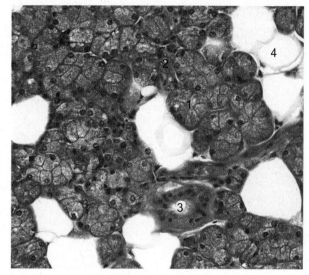

Fig. 15-1 Parotid gland (南方医 图)
1. serous acinus; 2. intercalated duct; 3. striated duct; 4. adipocyte

2) The striated ducts are wider and lined with simple columnar epithelial cells whose cytoplasm is eosinophilic.

3) The interlobulular ducts run between lobules; they are thicker and their lumens are lined by simple columnar or pseudostratified columnar epithelium.

2. Submandibular gland

Specimen No. _____ (see Fig. 2-8)

Preparation: HE stain

NE Similar to the general architecture of the parotid gland.

LMag Numerous serous, mucous and mixed acini as well as intercalated ducts and striated ducts can be seen in the lobules. The interlobular ducts can be found located between the lobules.

3. Pancreas

Specimen No. _____ Fig. 15-2, Fig. 15-3

Preparation: HE stain

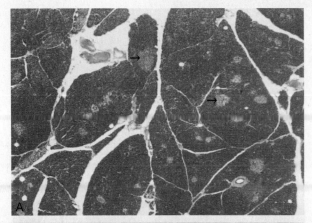

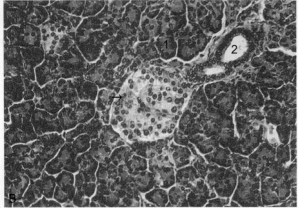

Fig. 15-2 Pancreas (复旦上医 图)
A. LMag. B. HMag. 1. serous acinus; 2. intralobular duct; → pancreatic islets

NE Similar to the parotid gland.
Microscope
(1) Capsule: It is a thin layer of connective tissue; it extends inward and separates the parenchyma into many lobules.
(2) Exocrine portion: It consists of closely packed serous acini and duct system. The intercalated ducts can be seen. The intralobular ducts, which are larger and surrounded by connective tissue, are lined by simple cuboidal epithelium. The epithelium of the interlobular ducts becomes columnar and they have even larger lumen.
(3) Pancreatic islets: The islets are small spherical pale stained clusters scattered among the acini. They vary in size. The islet cells are small, round, ovoid or polygonal in shape, with round or ovoid nucleus in the center and pink stained cytoplasm. Capillaries can be seen in the islets.

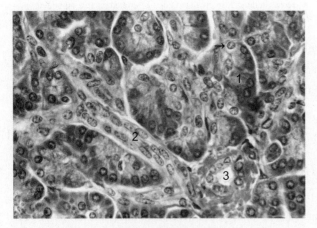

Fig. 15-3 The exocrine part of pancreas (南方医 图)
1. serous acinus; 2. intercalated duct; 3. intralobular duct; → centroacinar cells

4. Pig liver
Specimen No. _____ Fig. 15-4
Preparation: HE stain
NE One side of the specimen is covered by pink stained capsule; in the parenchyma, there are many polygonal hepatic lobules.
LMag
(1) Capsule: It constitutes of dense connective tissue invested by a layer of mesothelium. The connective tissue septa enter the parenchyma to divide the liver into clearly delimited lobules.
(2) Hepatic lobules: The hepatic lobules have various sections. Try to find a transverse polygonal section to observe.

1) The central veins: They locate in the center of the hepatic lobules and varied in size because of the orientations of cutting. Their walls are not discontinuous because of some sinusoids draining into the central veins.

2) Hepatic cords: Each cord consists of a row of closely packed hepatocytes. Hepatic cords are arranged more or less radially around the central vein. The hepatocytes in the peripheral portion of the lobules are a little smaller in size and a little stronger eosinophilic in staining, which form the limiting hepatic plates.

3) Sinusoids: They are situated between anastomosing and branching cords.

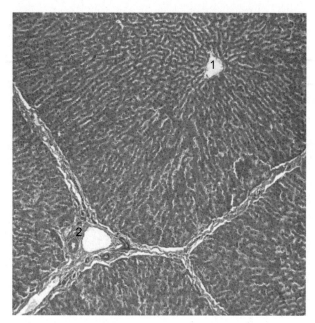

Fig. 15-4 Pig liver (南方医 图)
1. central vein; 2. portal area

(3) Portal areas: A portal area locates between two or three lobules; in the section there are more connective tissue and three parallel canals: the interlobular artery (branch of hepatic artery), interlobular vein (branch of portal vein) and the interlobular bile duct.

(4) Sublobular veins: They are small veins with larger lumen than the central veins.They run alone in the connective tissue of the non-portal areas.

5. Human liver

Specimen No. _____ Fig. 15-5 ~ Fig. 15-7

Preparation: HE stain

NE In the human liver, no clear boundary exists between the adjacent lobules.

LMag There is less connective tissue between the adjacent hepatic lobules, so no clear boundary exists among the neighboring lobules. Try to distinguish the central veins, hepatic cords, hepatic sinusoids, portal areas and sublobular veins.

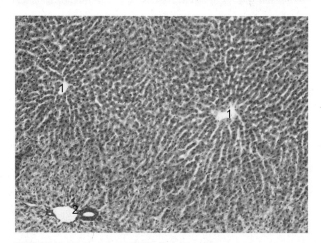

Fig. 15-5 Human liver (河北北方医 图)
1. central vein; 2. portal area

HMag

(1) Hepatocytes: They are large and polygonal shaped. They have one or two spherical nuclei with

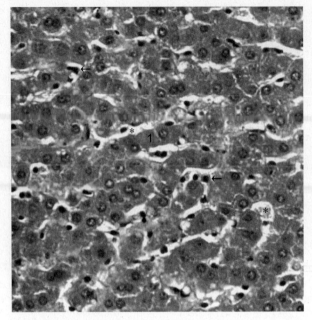

Fig. 15-6 Hepatic lobule (part) (南方医　图)
1. hepatic cord; * hepatic sinusoid; ← Kupffer cell

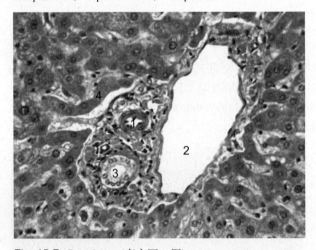

Fig. 15-7　Portal area (南方医　图)
1. interlobular artery; 2. interlobular vein; 3. interlobular bile duct;
4. limiting plate

clear nuclear membrane and prominent nucleoli. The cytoplasm is eosinophilic, but contains conspicuous basophilic bodies.

(2) Hepatic sinusoids: They occupy the spaces between the hepatic cords and have large and irregular lumens and discontinuous endothelium lining. Blood cells and Kupffer cells can be found in the lumen. The Kupffer cells are irregular shaped with dark nuclei and eosinophilic cytoplasm. They adhere to the endothelium quite often. The narrow space of Disse can be identified between the endothelium and the hepatic cord.

(3) Portal areas

1) The interlobular vein has a very thin wall and a large lumen lined by flattened endothelial cells. They can be found, in some areas, connected directly with the hepatic sinusoids.

2) The interlobular artery has a small round lumen with a few layers of circular arranged smooth muscle just outside the endothelium.

3) The interlobular bile duct is lined by simple cuboidal epithelium. The densely arranged cells have round and darkly stained nuclei and pale cytoplasm.

6. Kupffer cells (rat liver)

Specimen No. _____ Fig. 15-8

Preparation: Trypan blue or black ink injection via vein; hematoxylin stain

Microscope In the sinusoids, there are numerous Kupffer cells containing many trypan blue or black ink particles. The cells are irregular in shape with processes adhering to the endothelium. The prominent basophilic bodies and a few trypan blue particles can be found in the cytoplasm of the hepatocytes.

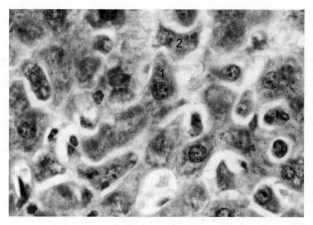

Fig. 15-8 Kupffer cells (rat liver; trypan blue injection, hematoxylin stain) (傅俊贤　图)

1. hepatocyte; 2. Kupffer cell

7. Glycogen of hepatocytes

Specimen No. _____ Fig. 15-9

Preparation: PAS reaction and hematoxylin stain

This preparation demonstrates the presence of the glycogen granules of hepatocyte, which being polysaccharide, PAS reaction-positive. So the granules are stained magenta. The nuclei are counterstained blue.

8. Bile canaliculi

Specimen No. _____ Fig. 15-10

Preparation: silver nitrate stain

This preparation demonstrates that bile canaliculi form a regular hexagonal network (stained brownish black) within each hepatic cord.

9. Blood vessels of the liver

Specimen No. _____ Fig. 15-11

Preparation: Perfusion of the blood vessels in the liver with carmine red gelatin or black ink

LMag The blood vessels are filled

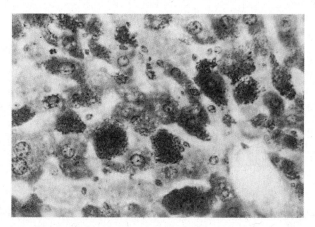

Fig. 15-9 Glycogen of hepatocytes (PAS reaction and hematoxylin stain) (复旦上医　图)

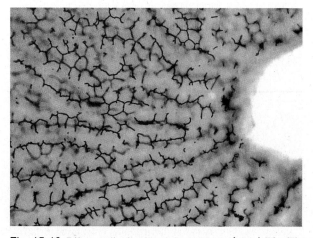

Fig. 15-10 Bile canaliculi (silver nitrate stain) (复旦上医　图)

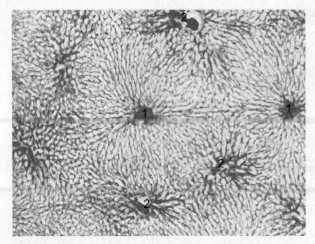

Fig. 15-11 Blood vessles of the liver (rat liver; perfusion of the blood vessles with carmine red gelatin) (吉大白医　图)
1. central vein; 2. portal area

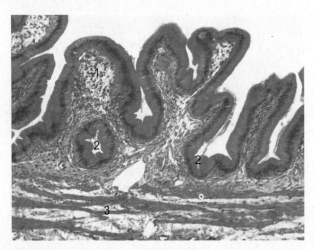

Fig. 15-12 Gall bladder (南方医　图)
1. mucosal fold; 2. mucous antrum; 3. muscularis

with red or black dye. The central veins, hepatic sinusoids, interlobular vessels and sublobular veins can be identified.

10. Gall bladder

Specimen No. _____ Fig. 15-12

Preparation: HE stain

NE One side of the section is the mucosa, which is uneven and blue stained; the rest part is pink stained.

LMag

(1) Mucous: The mucosa is thrown up into many branched folds, which are various in heights. The epithelium between the folds usually plunges into the lamina propria to form the mucous antrums. The mucosa of the gall bladder is made up of simple columnar epithelium; the lamina propria is thin, with a rich supply of blood vessels.

(2) Muscularis: Muscularis mucosa is not uniform in thickness and consists of irregularly oriented smooth muscles.

(3) Adventitia: The adventitia mucosa is well developed; most part of it is serous membrane.

(by Zhong Cuiping)

Chapter 16

Respiratory System

1. Olfactory region of the nose

Specimen No. _____ Fig. 16-1, Fig. 16-2

Preparation: HE stain

NE The specimen appears thin and long, the blue stained olfactory mucosa is located at the border, the osseous tissue in the deep.

LMag The epithelium of olfactory mucosa is pseudostratified columnar epithelium. In the connective tissue of the lamina propria, there are serous olfactory glands, blood vessels and nerve fiber bundles.

HMag Three types of cells can be identified in the epithelium according to the location and the shape of the nuclei. The contours and boundaries of the cells are not clear.

(1) Olfactory cells: They have large, round and pale stained nuclei at the middle of the epithelium.

(2) Supporting cells: They have smaller, oval and darkly stained nuclei, at the top or middle level.

(3) Basal cells: They have the smallest nuclei, which form a single layer at the base of the epithelium.

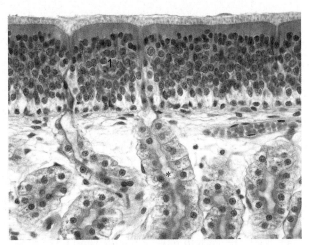

Fig. 16-1 Olfactory mucosa (周莉 图)

1. pseudostratified columnar epithelium; * olfactory gland

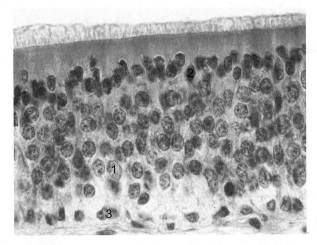

Fig. 16-2 Olfactory epithelium (周莉 图)

1. nucleus of olfactory cell; 2. nucleus of supporting cell; 3. nucleus of basal cell

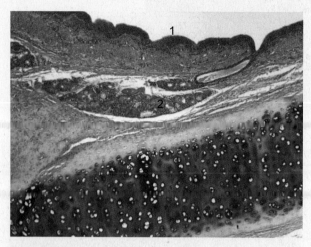

Fig. 16-3 Trachea (南方医　图)
1. epithelium; 2. tracheal gland; 3. hyaline cartilage

2. Trachea (TS)

Specimen No._____ Fig. 16-3

Preparation: HE stain

NE The luminal surface is the mucosa. The blue stained C-shaped structure is hyaline cartilage ring, the gap in the cartilage is the posterior wall of the trachea.

Microscope

(1) Mucosa: It is covered by pseudostratified ciliated columnar epithelium. Ciliated cells, goblet cells and basal cells can be identified. The basement membrane appears as a pink and thin band. In the connective tissue of the lamina propria, there are glandular ducts, many lymphocytes and small blood vessels.

(2) Submucosa: It consists of loose connective tissue and groups of serous or mucous acini. The submucosa and lamina propria shares a poorly defined border.

(3) Adventitia: It consists of loose connective tissue and a C-shaped hyaline cartilage ring. In the gap, there are smooth muscle bundles and mixed glands.

3. Lung

Specimen No. _____ Fig. 16-4 ~ Fig. 16-9

Preparation: HE stain

NE The smooth side of specimen is the capsule (serosa). Most of the specimen otherwise is the pulmonary respiratory portion, which looks like a meshwork.

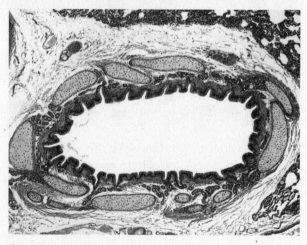

Fig. 16-4 Small bronchus (南方医　图)

LMag The serosa (at the smooth side) is composed of mesothelium and a thin layer of connective tissue. In the parenchyma, many pulmonary alveoli, some sections of small bronchi and their branches, some blood vessels can be observed.

(1) Small bronchus: Its lumen is the largest and its wall the thickest in the section. The mucosa is covered with pseudostratified ciliated columnar epithelium that contains some goblet cells. In the wall there are some discontinu-

ous bundles of smooth muscle, mixed glands and light blue stained cartilage plates.

(2) Bronchiole: A bronchiole has smaller lumen and thinner wall than the small bronchus. The mucosa may protrude into the lumen and form plica when the lumen becomes irregular. The epithelium of the bronchiole is simple columnar ciliated, containing a few goblet cells. In the wall, there are less or even no cartilage plates and glahds, but more circular smooth muscle.

(3) Terminal bronchiole: The lumen is much smaller and the epithelium is simple columnar, composed of Clara cells mainly, but no goblet cells. In the wall there is neither cartilage plate nor gland, while the smooth muscle forms a circular layer.

(4) Respiratory bronchiole: Its wall is interrupted by alveoli and lined by simple cuboidal epithelial cells and Clara cells.

(5) Alveolar duct: There are many openings of alveoli on its wall, so the incomplete wall presents as knobs between the openings. The knobs are lined by simple cuboidal or squamous epithelium. In the knob there is a small bundle of smooth muscle transversely sectioned.

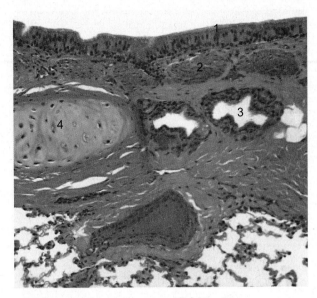

Fig. 16-5 Small bronchus (part) (南方医　图)
1. epithelium; 2. smooth muscle; 3. tracheal gland; 4. hyaline cartilage plate

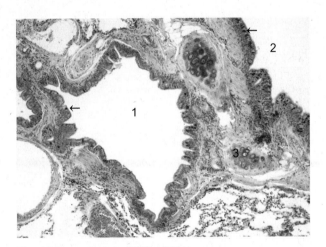

Fig. 16-6 Bronchiole (周莉　图)
1. bronchiole; 2. small bronchus (part); 3. hyaline cartilage plate; ← mucinogen granules (blue) in goblet cells

(6) Alveolar sac: It is the common central space toward which several alveoli open.

(7) Alveoli: The small sac-like structures in the section are alveoli. The tissue between the adjacent alveoli is the alveolar septum.

HMag

(1) Epithelium of alveoli: Type I cells are extremely attenuated cells that line the alveolar surfaces; they can only be identified by their flattened nuclei. Type II cells are round cells interspersed among the type I cells. They exhibit characteristic pale stained cytoplasm, large and round nuclei.

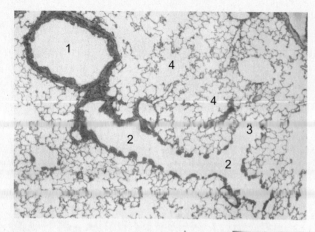

Fig. 16-7 Terminal bronchiole and the branches (南方医 图)
1. terminal bronchiole; 2. respiratory bronchiole;
3. alveolar duct; 4. alveolar sac

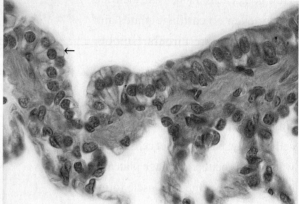

Fig. 16-8 The epithelium of terminal bronchiol (周莉 图)
← Clara cell

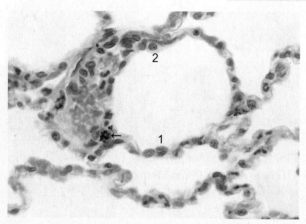

Fig. 16-9 Pulmonary alveoli (周莉 图)
1. type Ⅰ cell; 2. type Ⅱ cell; ← dust cell

(2) Alveolar septum: It is the tissue between the adjacent alveoli. Rich capillaries (containing red blood cells often), a few connective tissue and dust cells can be seen. The dust cells are present in both alveolar septum and alveolar lumen. These cells are large and oval or irregular shaped, containing more or less dark granules.

(3) Clara cells: Columnar Clara cells appear predominantly in the epithelium of terminal bronchiole. They are non-ciliated; the free surface appears prominent towards the lumen, and the cytoplasm is pale stained.

4. Elastic fibers in the lung

Specimen No. _____ Fig. 16-10

Preparation: Gomori's stain

Microscope Blue stained and very thin elastic fibers can be seen in the wall of the branches of bronchi and the alveolar septum.

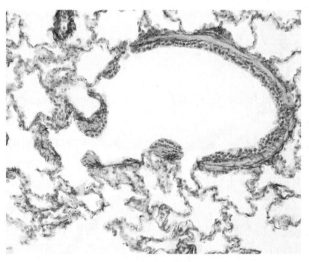

Fig. 16-10 Elstic fibers in lung (aldehyde-fuchsin stain showing the elastic fibers in blue) (周莉　图)

(by Zhou Li)

Chapter 17

Urinary System

1. Kidney

Specimen No. _____ Fig. 17-1 ~ Fig. 17- 4

Preparation: HE stain

NE Sectioned in pyramidal shape, the kidney consists of outer cortex and inner medulla. Renal corpuscles are dots in dark pink cortex, and the medullary pyramids are lighter. Arcuate arteries lie between the cortex and medulla.

LMag The cortex is doted with many renal corpuscles, which being adjacent to proximal convoluted tubule with darkly stained pink epithelium and distal convoluted tubule with pale stained epithelium. Parallel arrays of tubules, the medullary rays, penetrate the cortex. The medullary region has no renal corpuscle.

HMag

(1) Renal corpuscle: Each renal corpuscle consists of a tuft of capillaries, the glomerulus, surrounded by a double-walled epithelial capsule called glomerular capsule (Bowman's capsule). The external wall called the parietal layer has a simple squamous lining. The visceral lining of podocytes (inner wall) is too irregular to be seen clearly in light microscopy because it follows the curves of the individual capillaries. The urinary space is between the two walls. It is a fortune to

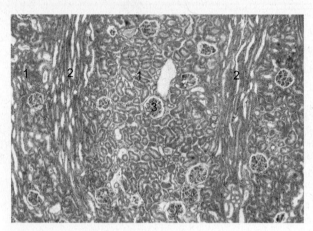

Fig. 17-1 Renal cortex (南方医 图)

1. cortical labyrinth; 2. medullary ray; 3. renal corpuscle

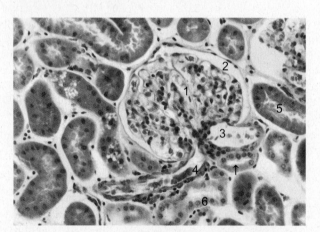

Fig. 17-2 Renal cortical labyrinth (河北北方医 图)

1. glomerulus; 2. cavity of renal capsule; 3. afferent arteriole; 4. efferent arteriole; 5. proximal convoluted tubule; 6. distal convoluted tubule; ↑ macula densa

have a section through the renal corpuscle that shows the vascular pole as well as the urinary pole. In most cases, either the vascular pole or the urinary pole is seen.

(2) Proximal convoluted tubules: More frequently seen near renal corpuscles in the renal cortex; it is lined with simple cuboidal epithelium or pyramidal epithelium with acidophilic cytoplasm and brush border.

(3) Distal convoluted tubules: They are light pink with low cuboidal epithelium lining without brush border.

(4) The juxtaglomerular apparatus: Some renal corpuscles are sectioned through the vascular pole; here the juxtaglomerular cells, macula densa, and extraglomerular mesangial cells can be seen. The macula densa appears as a closely packed group of epithelial cells lining the distal tubule. Juxtaglomerular cells would lie in the wall of the afferent arteriole. The triangular space just above the macula densa is filled with extraglomerular mesangial cells.

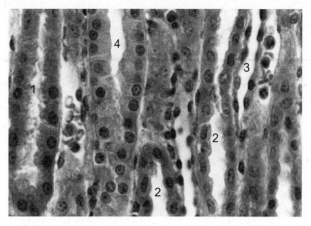

Fig. 17-3 Renal medulla (outer part, LS) (河北北方医　图)
1. proximal straight tubule; 2. distal straight tubule; 3. thin segment;
4. straight collecting duct

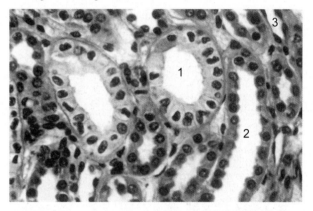

Fig. 17-4 Renal medulla (inner part, TS) (复旦上医　图)
1. straight collecting duct; 2. distal straight tubule; 3. thin segment

(5) Medulla: There are some longitudinal sections of pale collecting tubules. The epithelium of straight collecting tubules is regular simple columnar, with unusually clear cell outlines. Simple squamous lining indicates thin segments of loops of Henle. Compare these with capillaries. Brighter pink tubules are straight parts of proximal and distal tubules; these have histological resemblance to the convoluted portions of those tubules respectively.

2. Renal blood vessels

Specimen No.＿＿＿ Fig. 17-5

Preparation: Perfusion of renal blood vessels with carmine red gelatin or black ink, without staining of the sections.

LMag The lumens of blood vessels are filled with red or black dye. Arcuate arteries lie between the cortex and medulla. Interlobular arteries branch off from the arcuate arteries and follow a course in the cortex perpendicular to the renal capsule. From the interlobular arteries arise the

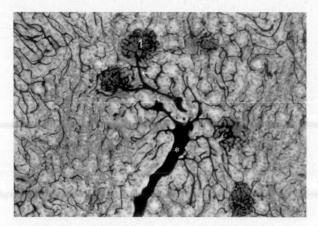

Fig. 17-5 Blood vessels in renal cortex (black ink perfusion via renal artery) (复旦上医　图)
1. glomerulus; * interlobular artery; ← afferent arteriole

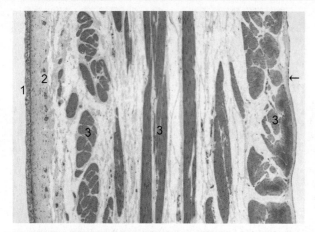

Fig. 17-6 Urinary bladder (南方医　图)
1. transitional epithelium; 2. connective tissue; 3. smooth muscle;
← mesothelium

afferent arterioles, which branch into the capillaries of the glomeruli. Blood passes from these capillaries into the efferent arterioles, which at once branch again to form a peritubular capillary network surrounding the proximal and distal tubules. Vasa recta follow a straight path into the medulla.

3. Urinary bladder

Specimen No. _____ Fig. 17-6 (see also Fig. 2-6, Fig. 2-7)

Preparation: HE stain

NE There are two sections on the slide, the thin one is the section of the wall of the distended bladder while the thick one is the section of the wall of the empty bladder.

Microscope The mucosa consists of a transitional epithelium and a lamina propria. Surrounding the lamina propria is a dense woven sheath of smooth muscle.

The transitional epithelium from empty urinary bladder contains 4 to 5 layers of cells; the superficial cells are large cuboidal and often bulge into the lumen.

The epithelium from the distended bladder is thin, only 2 to 3 cells thick, and the surface cells tend to be squamous.

(by Xu Chen)

Chapter 18

Male Reproductive System

1. Testis and epididymis

Specimen No. _____ Fig. 18-1 ~ Fig. 18-4

Preparation: HE stain

NE Notice the testis (generally, only part of the organ) sectioned with a small part of epididymis attached to it, and the pink mediastinal testis lying between them. The tunica albuginea covers the testis.

Testis

LMag The testis is covered by a thick capsule of dense connective tissue called the tunica albuginea. The existence of a large number of different sections of seminiferous tubules and the features of their walls show the different stages of spermatogenesis. Blood vessels and interstitial cells of Leydig lie in the connective tissue stroma between the tubules.

A few sections of tubuli recti can be seen in the area near the mediastinal testis. Its epithelium is low columnar without spermatogenic cells. The rete testis lies in the dense connective tissue of mediastinal testis. They are cavernous, irregular and low epithelium-lined channels.

HMag The small dark round nuclei along the base of the tubule belong to spermatogonia. Along the base can be seen large, pale, ovoid or triangular nuclei of Sertoli cells, each with a

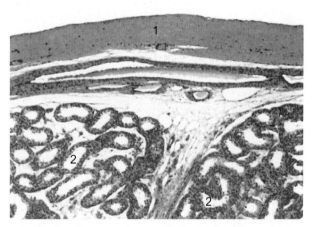

Fig. 18-1 Testis (复旦上医　图)
1. tunica albuginea; 2. seminiferous tubule

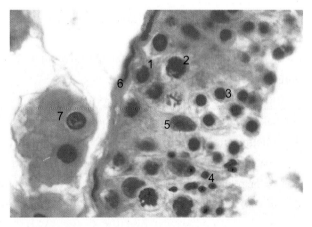

Fig. 18-2 Details of seminiferous tubule (复旦上医　图)
1. spermatogonium; 2. primary spermatocyte; 3. secondary spermatocyte; 4. spermatid; 5. Sertoli cell; 6. myoid cell; 7. Leydig cell

85

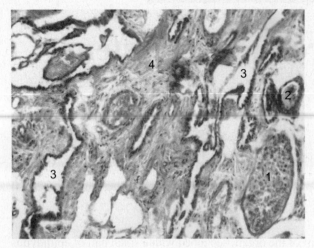

Fig. 18-3 Mediastinal testis (南方医　图)

1. seminiferous tubule; 2. tubulus rectus; 3. rete testis; 4. mediastinal testis

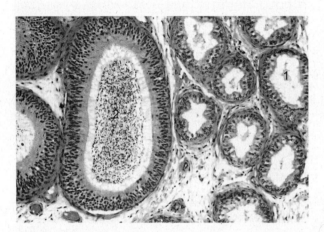

Fig. 18-4 Epididymis (上交大医　图)

1. efferent duct; 2. ductus epididymidis containing dense sperms

prominent nucleolus. The outlines of Sertoli cells appear poorly defined.

Primary spermatocytes have large nuclei with the dark, condensed chromosomes undergoing prophase of meiotic division; they lie just above the spermatogonia.

Secondary spermatocytes seldom can be seen in a section. Above the spermatocytes are round spermatids which can be distinguished by their small nuclei with areas of condensed chromatin. Their position within the seminiferous tubules is close to the lumen. Notice the differences between round early spermatids and elongated late spermatids.

Spermatozoon can be found in the lumen of the seminiferous tubules, with tails often cut out.

Clusters of Leydig cells lie in the interstitial tissue between the tubules. It is either round or ovoid in shape and has a central nucleus and strongly eosinophilic cytoplasm.

Epididymis

LMag The efferent ducts locate near the rete testis, the thickness of their epithelium is uneven, thus the lumen are irregular. The ductus epididymidis presents a regular epithelial border.

HMag The efferent ducts have an epithelium composed of groups of low nonciliated cuboidal cells alternating with high ciliated cells. These are motile cilia on the lining epithelium.

The ductus epididymidis is lined with pseudostratified columnar epithelium with stereocilia, composed of round basal cells and columnar cells, with some surrounding smooth muscle outside. Notice the regularity of the epithelium in height, which forms an unusually smooth apical line near the lumen.

2. Semen smear

Specimen No. _____ Fig. 18-5

Preparation: HE stain

Microscope A spermatozoon appears like a tadpole. The head is ovoid and stained blue, and the tail is long, thin and pink.

3. Prostate (sectioned through prostatic urethra)

Specimen No. _____ Fig. 18-6

Preparation: HE stain

NE The prostatic urethra is in the central part, and it is surrounded by secretory portions of the prostate.

Microscope The tubuloalveolar glands of the prostate are formed by cuboidal or columnar pseudostratified epithelium. Alveoli and ducts are not easily distinguished. Their lumens are irregular and wide generally Some concretions (homogeneous pink masses) can be seen in the lumen. An exceptionally rich fibromuscular stroma surrounds the glands.

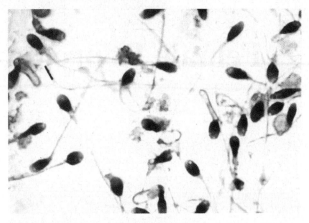

Fig. 18-5 Semen smear (上交大医　图)

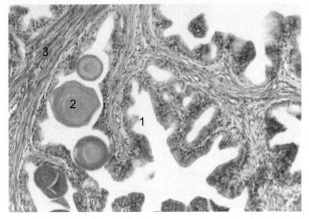

Fig. 18-6 Prostate (南方医　图)
1. acinus; 2. prostatic concretion; 3. smooth muscle

(by Xu Chen)

Chapter 19

Female Reproductive System

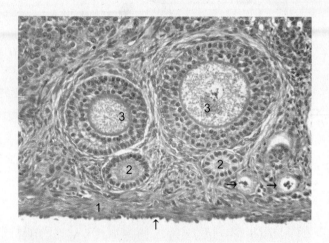

Fig.19-1 Ovary (cat) (南方医　图)

1. tunica albuginea; 2. primary follicle (early stage); 3. primary follicle (middle stage); ↑ germinal epithelium; → primordial follicle

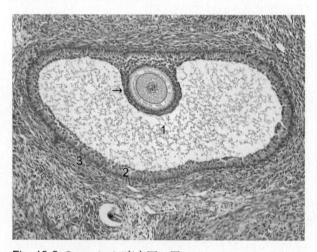

Fig. 19-2 Ovary (cat) (南方医　图)

1. follicular antrum; 2. stratum granulosum; 3. theca folliculi; * atretic follicle (remnant of zona pellucida); → cumulus oophorus

1. Ovary (cat or rabbit)

Specimen No. _____ Fig. 19-1 ~ Fig. 19-4

Preparation: HE stain

NE In the peripheral thick part, known as the cortex, we can see several ovarian follicles of unequal sizes, while the medulla is the narrow and the small part in the center. We can also find the structure called hilus ovarii, which attach to the mesovarium at one side in some samples.

LMag

(1) Capsule: The surface of an ovary is lined with a simple squamous or cuboidal epithelium, the germinal epithelium. Beneath it is a thin layer of dense connective tissue, the tunica albuginea, which is not obvious.

(2) Cortex: It contains follicles at different stages of development, the atretic follicles, the corpus luteum and the corpus albicans. The connective tissue between these structures may contain fusiform stroma cells.

(3) Medulla: There is no sharp boundary between the cortical and the medullary regions. In the loose connective tissue there are abundant blood vessels and lymphatic vessels. A small number of hilus cells, structurally similar to the testicular interstitial cells, can be seen at the peri-hilar region.

HMag

(1) Primordial follicles: Many small primordial follicles are located at the superficial layer of the cortex. There is a big round primary oocyte in its center, and its nucleus is big and round, pale stained, with a clear nucleolus. The cytoplasm is weakly eosinophilic. The primary oocyte is surrounded by a layer of flat follicular cells with no obvious boundary between them; we can only see their ovoid nuclei.

(2) Primary follicles: The primary follicles are larger than primordial follicles. They consist of the following structures.

1) Primary oocyte: It is in the center and is bigger than those in the primordial follicles.

2) Follicular cells: They are cuboidal or columnar, and are in one layer or multiple layers. Some small intercellular lacunae may appear between follicular cells.

3) Corona radiata: It is a layer of radiating columnar follicular cells which surround the oocyte tightly.

4) Zona pellucida: Zona pellucida is a layer of homogeneous and eosinophilic membrane between the oocyte and corona radiata.

(3) Secondary follicles: They are much bigger than primary follicles. Some structures appear at this stage.

1) Follicular antrum: It is a big crescentic lumen. We can see pink floccule in it, which is formed by solidified protein of the follicular fluid.

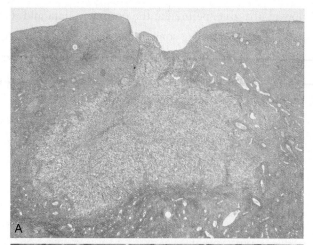
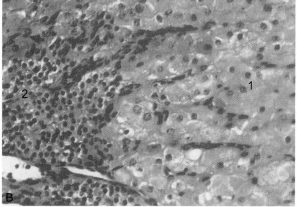

Fig. 19-3 Corpus luteum (A. 南方医 B. 复旦上医 图)
A. LMag. B. HMag. 1. granular lutein cell; 2. theca lutein cell

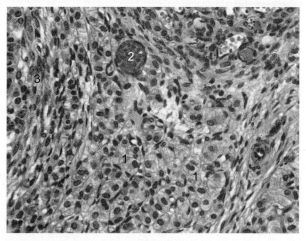

Fig. 19-4 Interstitial gland (南方医 图)
1. interstitial gland; 2. venule; 3. stroma

2) Cumulus oophorus: It is the eminence towards the follicular antrum, and contains the primary

oocyte, the zona pellucida, the corona radiata and its peripheral follicular cells. Due to the direction of sectioning, some follicles appear with a large follicular antrum and partial cumulus oophorus, and no oocyte can be seen.

3) Stratum granulosum: It consists of several layers of densely packed follicular cells (granulosa cells), which constitute the wall of the follicle.

4) Theca folliculi: It is just outside the follicle. It includes the theca interna and the theca externa. The theca cells of the former, with round nuclei and eosinophilic cytoplasm are relatively large and polygonal. The latter consists mainly of smooth muscle fibers.

(4) Premature follicle: It is very large and near the ovarian surface. Both the primary oocyte and the follicular antrum are big. The stratum granulosum is thin and the zona pellucida is thick. The attachment between the stratum granulosum and cumulus oophorus is narrow. (It is hard to see a mature follicle in the sample since it is discharged quickly).

(5) Atretic follicles: The follicles at any stage of development may undergo atresia and there are a lot of morphological differences between various stages of follicular development and the atretic course. At early stage, we can find the karyopyknosis of primary oocytes and apoptotic bodies of follicular cells (nuclear debris with strongly basophilic stain). Moreover, macrophages and neutrophils appear within follicles. At later stage, only an irregular ring of the zona pellucida can be seen.

(6) Corpus luteum: (It cannot be found in all samples because of the sex cycle of the animals). It is a large yellowish-pink stained cell mass.

1) Granulosa lutein cells: They appear as many large polygonal cells located in the center. The round nuclei are located in the center of the cell. The cytoplasm is pink and contains small vacuolar lipid droplets.

2) Theca lutein cells: They are less and smaller than granulosa lutein cells. They are mainly located in the periphery. Their cell bodies are irregular and both cytoplasm and nuclei are stained intensely.

(7) Interstitial glands: There are a lot of interstitial glands dispersed in the ovaries of cats and rabbits. The interstitial gland cells form masses or cordlike structures. The cells are big and polygonal. The nuclei are round and the cytoplasm contains lipid droplets.

2. Oviduct (TS)

Specimen No. ____ Fig. 19-5, Fig. 19-6

Preparation: HE stain

NE There are many folds at the luminal surface. The blue stained part is the

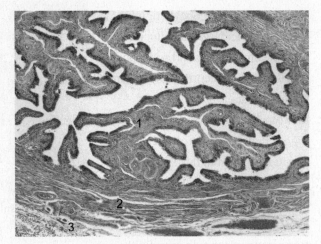

Fig. 19-5 Oviduct (ampulla) (南方医 图)
1. mucosa fold; 2. muscular layer; 3. serosa (connective tissue)

mucosa and the peripheral pink part is the rest of the oviduct wall.

Microscope

(1) Mucosa: There are numerous folds with branches that project into the lumen. The mucosa is composed of a simple columnar epithelium and a lamina propria composed of loose connective tissue. The epithelium contains two types of cells, i.e., ciliated cells and secretory cells. The ciliated cells have cilia on the free surface, and the nuclei are round or ovoid and the cytoplasm is weakly eosinophilic. The secretory cells are smaller and are located between the ciliated cells. Their elliptical nuclei are deeply stained and the cytoplasm is strongly eosinophilic.
(2) Muscular layer: The thick muscularis is composed of smooth muscles disposed as an inner circular or spiral and an outer longitudinal layer.
(3) Serosa: It is composed of visceral peritoneum.

3. Uterus (proliferative phase)

Specimen No. _____ Fig. 19-7, Fig. 19-8
Preparation: HE stain
NE The endometrium is the surface layer which is stained blue; the myometrium is the thick layer which is stained pink.

Microscope The uterus wall has three layers：endometrium, myometrium, and serosa.
(1) Endometrium
1) Its simple columnar epithelium is formed by a large amount of secretory cells and sporadic ciliated cells.

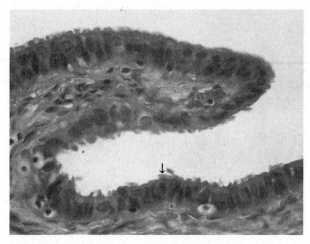

Fig. 19-6 Epithelium of oviduct (南方医　图)
↓ ciliated cell

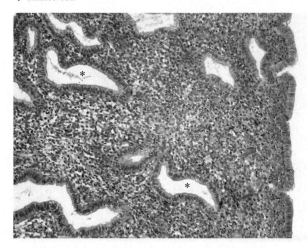

Fig. 19-7 Uterus (proliferative phase) (南方医　图)
* uterine gland

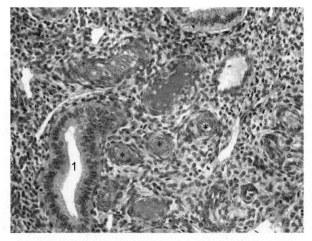

Fig. 19-8 Uterus (proliferative phase) (南方医　图)
1. uterine gland; * coiled artery

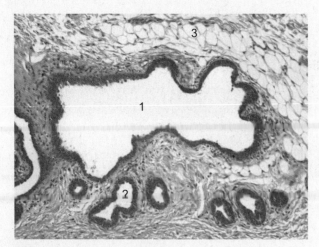

Fig. 19-9 Mammary gland (quiescent phase) (南方医　图)
1. duct; 2. alveolus; 3. adipose tissue

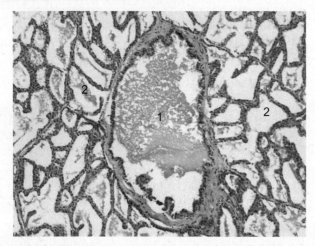

Fig. 19-10 Mammary gland (active phase) (南方医　图)
1. duct; 2. alveolus

2) The lamina propria: Its connective tissue contains many stroma cells and a few fibers. The uterine glands are straight or a little tortuous and the gland lumens are narrow. If you find several consecutive arterioles in cross sections, of course, you can consider them as coiled arterioles.

(2) Myometrium: It is the thickest tunic and composed of many bundles of smooth muscle fibers separated by connective tissue. Some thick blood vessels can be seen.

(3) Serosa.

4. Mammary glands (quiescent stage)

Specimen No. _____ Fig. 19-9，Fig. 19-10

Preparation: HE stain

NE The epidermis is the blue stained part at one side of the sample. Lobules of mammary glands are the small blue clumps distributed in the pink tissues.

Microscope

Mammary glands of quiescent stage are characterized by a small quantity of glandular tissue among the connective and the adipose tissue. A few alveoli can be seen in the lobules and they have simple cuboidal or columnar epithelium. Moreover, the lumens of the alveoli are narrow and sometimes they are just a cell mass without lumen. It is difficult to distinguish alveoli from intralobular ducts. But the interlobular and common ducts have wide lumens; their walls are composed, in order of simple columnar, stratified columnar and stratified squamous epithelium, as the ducts approaching the epidermis.

(by Wang Zhanyou)